P.B

'I need a wife,

'Emma needs tw
equally, and it seer
'that there's only one solution.'

Roxy held her breath.

'If you and I were to marry, Roxy, it would solve both our dilemmas,' Cam said coolly.

He might have been a hard-headed executive proposing a business merger. As a marriage proposal, it lacked a lot.

Except maybe a glimmer of sense.

That was Roxy's initial reaction, until the reality hit her like a thunderbolt. Cam Raeburn was asking her to marry him! Feelings, emotions would play no part in this 'suitable' marriage he was proposing. How could she plunge into such a cold-hearted, loveless arrangement and expect it to work? Even for her niece's sake, the price would be too high!

Instantly she felt a rush of shame. No price would be too high when it came to her sister's baby. She'd do anything—anything—to give back to her niece the love and security that poor little Emma had lost...

Elizabeth Duke was born in Adelaide, South Australia, but has lived in Melbourne all her married life. She trained as a librarian and has worked in many different types of libraries, but she was always secretly writing. Her first published book was a children's novel, after which she successfully tried her hand at romance writing. She has since given up her work as a librarian to write romance full-time. When she isn't writing or reading, she loves to travel with her husband John, either within Australia or overseas, gathering inspiration and background material for future romances. She and John have a married son and daughter, who now have children of their own.

Recent titles by the same author:

THE HUSBAND DILEMMA

THE PARENT TEST

BY
ELIZABETH DUKE

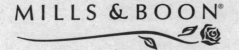

MILLS & BOON®

First published in Great Britain 1999
Harlequin Mills & Boon Limited,
Eton House, 18-24 Paradise Road, Richmond, Surrey TW9 1SR

© Elizabeth Duke 1999

ISBN 0 263 81888 8

Set in Times Roman 10½ on 12¼ pt.
02-9912-47131 C1

Printed and bound in Spain
by Litografía Rosés, S.A., Barcelona

CHAPTER ONE

ROXY'S nerves were strung tight by the time her plane touched down in Sydney after the long flight from Los Angeles. Her emotions were swinging from joyful anticipation at the thought of seeing her baby niece again, for only the second time, to a shivery dread at the prospect of coming face to face again with Cam Raeburn, the man she was prepared to fight for custody of her niece.

Nobody was at the airport to meet her, which didn't surprise her. Nobody but her father knew that she was arriving back in Australia today, and he was living in Western Australia now, with Roxy's stepmother Blanche. Crabby old Blanche had wanted to live near her own daughter's family, as far away from her husband's family as possible.

And now that Roxy's sister Serena and brother-in-law Hamish had tragically gone, Blanche was doing her best to sever all ties with her remaining stepdaughter—and the orphaned baby girl Hamish and Serena had left behind.

'No, of course the baby's not with us!' Blanche had squawked when Roxy had called from northern Mexico after hearing the shocking news of the tragic boating accident. 'How could I take care of a baby with my arthritis? And your father has a bad heart, remember? Don't worry, the child's in good hands. Hamish's brother, Cam Raeburn, is looking after her.'

Roxy wouldn't have wanted Blanche taking care of her baby niece anyway, even temporarily. Even Cam Raeburn was preferable to Blanche. As the baby's uncle and godfather, Cam should at least have his niece's best interests at heart.

Roxy humphed as she hailed a cab to her Sydney flat. Best interests or not, she had to make Cam see that *she* was the best one to take care of their niece from now on. She was Serena's sister—the baby's aunt—while he was a single *man*…a divorcee…a womanising bachelor who surely wouldn't want to be lumbered with a baby indefinitely.

With a bit of luck the novelty of looking after his seven-month-old niece was already wearing off.

She hoped so—fervently. It would make things so much easier and less traumatic for the baby if he would simply hand their niece over. Once she had little Emma safely back here in Sydney, she would apply for formal custody.

It didn't take long to reach her two-bedroomed flat in suburban Coogee—the flat where she'd be bringing baby Emma soon, hopefully. As she carried her bags into her bedroom Roxy caught sight of herself in the full-length mirror.

She looked a fright. She couldn't let Cam see her like this!

Her cotton top was like a crumpled rag. Her old faded jeans had stains from the coffee she'd spilt on the plane. And her short-cropped hair, normally sunbleached and glowing with natural golden highlights, looked dull and drab and even more of a mess than usual.

She always wore her hair short, in a naturally tousled style—with her fine-boned face and slight build it suited her best that way and was easier to manage. But her new choppy hairstyle had short jagged bits sticking out all over. The nursing aide who'd cut it for her at the hospital in Los Angeles had called it a 'dishevelled bob', supposedly the latest trend in L.A. salons.

As her gaze settled on her drawn face, Roxy sighed. Normally tanned and healthy, she looked thin and pale after her three-week stay in hospital, and the long flight had left her blue eyes darkly shadowed and lacking their usual lustre.

She fingered her bottom lip tentatively. At least the surgery on her mouth had had time to heal…thanks to that ghastly virus which had kept her in hospital for an additional two long weeks. In fact, the extra time in hospital had been a blessing in another way too. It had given her time to mourn Serena and Hamish…time to recover from her grief and shock before coming home to face further trauma in the shape of Cam Raeburn.

Before taking a quick shower and changing into a fresh shirt and jeans, she called her father to let him know she was back and that she was planning to head down the coast to Raeburns' Nest to claim her niece.

'I'm home to take care of Emma now,' she told him firmly.

'Oh, Roxy, love, how can you look after a baby?' Her father sounded frailer each time she talked to him. Part sorrow at losing a daughter, and part Blanche, Roxy thought with a grimace. Her stepmother would wear anyone out.

'She'll be better off with me than with Cam Raeburn,' she insisted.

'But you're always away in some far-flung country, love. Emma would be stuck alone in your flat for months at a time and it would cost you a fortune in baby-sitters. How could you afford it? At least with Cam Raeburn caring for her, Emma will have an uncle and a live-in nanny with her all the time. And with his wealth, Cam can afford a daily housekeeper and every possible luxury.'

A live-in nanny…a daily housekeeper…every possible luxury. Roxy's heart dipped.

'And now that Cam owns Raeburns' Nest,' her father ploughed on, 'he's able to keep Emma in her own home, in familiar surroundings. With a rich uncle like Cam Raeburn, love, the baby won't want for anything.'

Roxy pulled a face. 'Anything but a mother.'

'Roxy, love, with your field trips…'

'I'll give up my field work! I'll try to get extra teaching hours at Uni. They have a creche there now.' But the long summer break had just started at Uni and lectures didn't resume until next March—four months away. 'I'll manage,' she asserted, but her voice wavered. Whether she gave up her field work to stay at home all the time or not, how could she compete with what Cam Raeburn had to offer Emma?

'You'd better have it out with Cam.' Her father sighed. 'I don't think he'll be prepared to give her up.'

'Once he knows that I'm back and that I'm prepared to—'

'He's planning to get married again, love. He told

me when I called him the other day to ask after Emma. He wants to give the baby a proper family again, he said, like she had with Hamish and Serena.'

Shock jolted Roxy into silence for several long seconds. *Getting married again? Cam Raeburn?*

'He wants to *marry* one of his flashy bimbo brunettes?' she finally bit out. She felt a trembling, irrational surge of fury. 'I'll fight him in the courts first!'

Her father gave a brief, sympathetic laugh. 'A single, penniless female, fighting a rich industrial chemist with a highly profitable business and powerful connections? And a married man?'

'He's not married yet! And if I have anything to do with it, I'll have poor little Emma out of his clutches before he is! Serena wanted *me* to have Emma,' Roxy burst out. 'She told me once that if anything ever happened to them, she wanted me to bring up their daughter!'

'Serena—um—didn't mention custody in her will, love…unfortunately. Look…you'd better take that up with Cam as well.'

'Oh, I will, don't worry.' Her voice trembled. She'd have a lot of things to take up with Cam Raeburn when she saw him. But first she had to find out more about this woman he was planning to marry. As a married man—as a wealthy husband with a wife—he'd hold every trump card. She'd have no hope in the world of fighting him and winning.

Had he actually *proposed* yet? Or was he just thinking about it?

A bitter memory stirred, and she shivered. The night of her sister's wedding…Cam Raeburn, leading

her into that secluded moonlit garden…the deceptive
magic in the air… She swallowed hard, remembering
the way he'd kissed her, soaring her to heights she'd
never known…the way he'd looked at her, gazing
deep into her eyes…the way he'd murmured, in that
deep rumbling voice of his, *Things can happen when
you least expect them to.*

How prophetic his words had been! When *she'd*
least expected it, the magic spell he'd been weaving
had cruelly shattered. The moment Cam had found
out that she wasn't just a history lecturer, but also an
archeologist who spent half her year out of Australia,
scrabbling around in the dirt at remote digs, he'd lost
interest in her. Worse, he'd dumped her for someone
else. A stunning dark-eyed brunette.

Hurt, humiliated and angry, she'd been trying to
avoid him ever since. They'd only come face to face
once in the past year and a half…unavoidably, at
baby Emma's christening five months ago, when their
niece was just two months old. In typical fashion,
Cam had flaunted another raven-haired beauty in her
face—a clone of the one at her sister's wedding.

She hadn't been back home since—until now.

Who was this girl Cam was planning to marry?

Had Cam Raeburn finally found a leggy, dark-eyed
brunette who was willing to look after a home and a
baby? Was he so determined to give his niece a secure, stable family life again that he'd decided to
marry his niece's *nanny?*

No! Roxy thought violently, her face heating.
Serena's baby is *not* going to be brought up by a
roving-eyed uncle and some flashy bimbo who
doesn't genuinely care about her. Emma is *my* re-
sponsibility.

She drew in her lips, her eyes narrowing as she asked her father caustically, 'Emma's live-in nanny wouldn't happen to be a young, stunning-looking brunette, by any chance?'

'Young? A brunette? *Mary?*' Her father gave a confused laugh. 'No, love, Mary's a widowed grandmother—a former mothercraft nurse. She used to mind the baby for Serena and Hamish when they wanted an evening out or at weekends when they went sai—' He stopped, choking on the word 'sailing'.

Roxy swiftly changed tack. 'Well, I'm sure Cam won't want to be left holding the baby for too long.' It would cramp his style too much. 'Not that he'll need to, now that I'm home.' Her spirits had lifted a little. At least it wasn't the live-in nanny.

'Roxy...' It was Blanche's voice on the phone now, sharp and impatient as always. 'You're tiring your father. It's time for his rest.'

'I have to go anyway. Tell Dad to take care.' Roxy hung up and started dialling the number of Raeburns' Nest.

She was familiar with the number because Hamish and Serena had lived there during their idyllic, far-too-short marriage. Now Cam, it seemed, had moved back into his old family home. It belonged to him now.

She'd only spoken to Cam once since the tragedy six weeks ago, when she'd called him from northern Mexico after speaking to her father—and only after learning that Cam had temporary custody of the baby.

The line had been shocking, full of static, and she'd had to shout. 'Cam? It's Roxy Warren.'

'Well...Roxy.' She'd felt the chill in his voice even over that very noisy, distorted line. 'You couldn't even come home for your sister's funeral. We thought a week's notice would have been ample, even for you.'

A burst of ear-splitting static had muffled her indignant reply: 'I've only just heard. I've been camping out in northern Mexico for the past—'

But Cam was speaking over her, his words cracking like gunfire down the fast-disintegrating line. 'Your father could have done with your support at the funeral. Blanche was no—' He swore, and gave up. 'Look, this line's impossible. Hang up and call your father. He'll be back in Perth by now.'

'I've already—' But the line had gone dead.

Even now, anger surged inside her at the memory. She could have done with a little sympathy, not a barrage of unfair criticism. She hadn't even had a chance to ask after her niece, let alone let Cam know that she was on her way home to take care of the baby.

Her unlucky accident on arriving in Los Angeles the next day—and the bug that had hit her days later in the hospital—had prevented her from making any more calls. She'd managed to send word to her father, via one of the nurses, and had eventually spoken to him herself before leaving the hospital.

But she'd made no attempt to call Cam Raeburn again until now. She hadn't wanted to warn him that she was about to leave hospital and come home. She didn't trust him.

She had good reason not to trust him.

CHAPTER TWO

HER hand shook as she held the phone to her ear, waiting for an answer.

'Cam Raeburn.'

Her stomach knotted. 'Hullo, Cam, it's Roxy. I'm back and I'd like to come down to Raeburns' Nest to see Emma,' she said breathlessly, before he had a chance to cut in.

She didn't like the pause that followed. 'By all means,' he agreed finally. 'Why don't you pack an overnight bag and stay for the weekend? If you can spare a whole weekend with your niece.'

She gritted her teeth, even as her heart jumped in panic at the thought of staying under the same roof as Cam Raeburn for a whole weekend. 'I have all the time in the world,' she assured him loftily. 'My niece is my top priority from now on.'

And I'll stay at Raeburns' Nest for as long as it takes to convince you of that, she added under her breath. If she hoped to convince him that she was the best person to look after Emma, she would have to use the utmost care and tact…and be prepared to stay for however long it took.

'Is it all right if I come now? This afternoon?' she asked in a less confrontational tone. Sleeping off her jet lag would have to wait.

'We'll be here. You can remember where to come?'

She scowled at the implication that she'd seldom been home to visit her family. 'I'll find it,' she ground out. She'd only been to Raeburns' Nest once before…on the day of Emma's christening five months ago, on her last visit home. Serena and Hamish had invited everyone back to their home after the simple ceremony at their local church.

As she showered and changed, Roxy brooded on the unwanted encounter.

There'd been no avoiding Cam in the tiny coastal church. As godmother and godfather to baby Emma, they'd had to stand side by side at the font.

Cam hadn't changed a bit in the twelve months that had passed since Serena's wedding. Still as good-looking as ever, as sexy as ever. The same tall, athletic build…the same amazing shoulders…the same shiny dark hair…the same glittering black eyes…but the softness she'd once seen in them had gone.

He'd been the first to break the ice. Every painful word, every charged look, was etched in her memory.

'Back for long this time, Roxy?'

She bristled at his tone, at the cynically raised eyebrow. A year might have passed, but obviously nothing had changed. She'd thought for a fleeting second, as their eyes briefly met, that a spark had leapt to life in the lethal black depths, but it was gone in a flash.

His normal reaction to a woman—any woman, no doubt—until he'd remembered who she was. A foot-loose, scruffy-haired history freak who liked fossicking in the heat and dust in remote corners of the world, unearthing ancient civilisations.

'I'll be going away again sooner than I expected,' she hissed back at him, tossing her head to show him she couldn't wait to go—while wishing at the same time that she'd worn something a little more sophisticated to her niece's christening than a longsleeved granny dress, straw hat and flatheeled shoes.

'There's been an exciting new find in the far north of Mexico,' she crisply informed him, 'and I've been invited to join the team there. I'm leaving next week.'

Despite the coolness between them, her body was reacting to his nearness, her nerve-ends quivering, her skin heating. It was *his* fault she'd decided to go away again so soon, *his* fault she'd extended her field trips since her sister's wedding. If Cam's passionate kisses had genuinely meant something...if he'd *asked* her to stay...if he'd *wanted* her to stay... But he hadn't. He'd preferred the dark-eyed brunette.

He'd even brought another flashing-eyed bimbo to his niece's christening!

'Roxy...I don't believe you've met Belinda.' Cam's eyes hadn't even flickered as he'd introduced her to his latest dark-eyed stunner. 'Belinda's a member of my tennis club, back in Sydney.'

I bet you've done more than played tennis together, Roxy had thought nastily, noting the woman's luscious red lips and provocative smile. A real *femme fatale*. Just Cam's type.

The type who would never have dirty fingernails or a hair out of place.

She sighed. Tousle-haired, blue-eyed blondes with an odd dress sense and a craze for ancient civilizations were obviously not Cam's type.

Roxy dismissed the galling memory, sighing heavily as she threw clothes into a bag—enough for a week or longer—then jumped into her car for the two-hour drive south. She wondered if the dark-eyed Belinda was still around. Or was there yet another ravishing brunette? Ravishing enough for Cam to want to marry?

It was a slow trip out of the city, and there was heavy traffic on the freeway south. After a trying hour and a half, she caught a glimpse of the coast, and the sprawling industrial city of Wollongong, where Cam's flourishing chemical and fibremaking plant was, as well as his head office and a company house where he could stay if he wished. She knew that he also had a marketing office in Sydney—and a city penthouse.

She blew out a sigh. How could she compete with all that?

After another half an hour she saw the long sweep of the coast again, and the popular coastal township of Kiama, where her brother-in-law, Hamish, had co-owned a pharmacy.

Roxy gulped down a lump in her throat, still finding it hard to believe that Hamish and Serena had gone. They'd been so perfect for each other, so happy together. They'd shared everything. Even—tragically—a love of sailing.

Blinking away a blur of tears, she turned her thoughts to their baby daughter, wondering how her niece was getting on with Cam Raeburn—a very different type of man from the baby's gentle, home-loving father, Hamish. Emma had been with Cam for six weeks now. Had they bonded in that time? Would the baby be upset, all over again, if she took her away from him?

Raeburns' Nest was a few kilometers further down

the coast, perched high on the rich green cliffs over-looking the ocean. Hamish and Cam had jointly in-herited the family home on the death of their wid-owed father. The two brothers had shared the house until Cam married his wife, Kimberley, and built a new home in the lush Kangaroo Valley nearby—a house he'd sold after his divorce, moving back into his Sydney apartment and his company house at Wollongong. Hamish had stayed on at Raeburns' Nest, bringing his beloved bride, Serena, to live there with him after their whirlwind two-month courtship.

Roxy's hands began to tremble as the house came into view. Set in a couple of acres of natural bush, the big old sandstone house looked even more com-fortably imposing then the last time she'd seen it, now that the new guest wing, which Hamish had been building on at the time, was complete. As she swung her baby Mazda into the gravel drive alongside the house, she caught a glimpse of the tree-lined tennis court and fenced in-ground swimming pool to the rear of the house, framed by trees, lawn and thick bush.

An ideal home for bringing up a family, she mused with a sigh, her spirits nosediving. How could her two-bedroomed city flat compete with a home like this? With luxury like this?

Dragging her bag from the rear seat, and the giant teddy bear she'd bought for the baby at L.A. airport, she followed a brick-paved path to the side door, avoiding the formal front entrance overlooking the cliffs.

She expected to see Cam's housekeeper appear when she knocked, or even Mary, the nanny, but it was Cam himself who opened the door.

For a stunned second she stood staring at him, unable to speak. He looked so vastly different from her remembered image of him. On the only two occasions she'd met him before he'd been dressed to the nines—in formal black tie at Serena's wedding, and twelve months later, at Emma's christening, in a stylish grey suit, neat white shirt and red silk tie.

On both occasions his thick dark hair had been neatly slicked back and shiny clean, his handsome, strong-jawed face clean-shaven, his powerful shoulders enhanced by the superb cut of his jacket.

Today he was wearing frayed denim shorts and a faded T-shirt with food stains down the front. His strong face was shadowed with overnight growth, his thick hair uncombed, looking as if he'd just climbed out of bed, and his long tanned feet were bare, with an orange splotch on one of them.

She felt almost overdressed, for once, in her washed-out blue jeans, long-sleeved white shirt, loosely knotted at the waist, and well-worn sneakers.

Yet—she swallowed hard—his appearance didn't repel her, as it should have. He looked incredibly, heart-stoppingly sexy.

As if realising he was under scrutiny, Cam's mouth curved in a face-crinkling smile that was part mocking, part rueful.

'I haven't had time to shave yet, though I did manage a quick shower, after the baby threw up all over me. Lunchtime was interesting too...' He brushed a hand over his stained T-shirt. 'This *was* a clean shirt until Emma made it clear she doesn't like mashed pumpkin. I'm on my own this weekend,' he explained. 'I gave Mary the weekend off to visit her family, and Philomena doesn't come at weekends.'

Philomena, Roxy assumed, was his housekeeper. Since she wasn't around at weekends, she was unlikely to be one of his bimbos!

'You're finding our niece a handful?' she asked hopefully. If he was complaining already, it shouldn't be too difficult to persuade him to hand Emma over.

'Even the best *mothers* find babies a handful at times,' he said dryly. 'Come in, Roxy, I'll show you to your room. You can see Emma later. She's asleep at the moment and I don't believe in waking a sleeping baby unnecessarily.'

Roxy bit her tongue, tempted as she was to protest at the implication that she was unnecessary. He was quite right not to wake the baby. Even if his motive might be suspect.

As he closed the door behind her he studied her face for a disconcerting few seconds. She sucked in a breath as strong warm fingers closed round her chin, tilting her face upward.

'Well...they certainly did a good job.' His tone was faintly caustic. Not a hint of sympathy. He drew back, letting her go as if the very touch of her repulsed him. 'Though why in hell's name you'd want to have cosmetic surgery in the first place, let alone now, when you could have been here at home comforting your father or your sister's baby...well, it leaves me baffled. And disgusted, frankly.'

Her jaw dropped. 'You think—'

'Well, okay...so you were already in hospital with some virus—fair enough—but don't deny you used

the opportunity to have a little nip and a tuck while
you were recuperating in that L.A. hospital.'

Roxy's chest heaved, her breath coming in furious
gulps. 'Who—told—you—that?' she managed to
gasp out.

'Your father told me...no, Blanche. Blanche, cutting in on poor old George, as usual.' The corner of
his lip quirked. He shared her opinion of Blanche.
The only thing they did share, though she'd hoped at
one time—a fleeting, futile hope—that they might one
day share other things, too.

'She told me, quite clearly, that you were having
cosmetic surgery on your face,' Cam said flatly.

Jealous, bitchy Blanche...Roxy's hands balled into
fists. 'I didn't have cosmetic surgery,' she ground out.
'I had *micro*surgery. To repair a wound. Trust
Blanche to get it wrong.' Deliberately, if she knew
Blanche.

He cocked an eyebrow at her. 'Microsurgery? A
wound? Where?' Again she had to suffer his scrutiny,
his gaze searing into her already flushed skin.

She swallowed. 'On my mouth. My lower lip. I
tripped over a street kerb as I jumped out of a car in
L.A. to rush into a shop. I crashed headfirst onto a
concrete plant pot.'

'You were gallivanting around LA, *shopping,* after
hearing the news of your sister's death?' Cam shook
his head, cold contempt in his eyes. 'Your father sent
you an urgent fax six *weeks* ago, while you were still
in northern Mexico. You sure were in no hurry to
come home!'

She glared at him. 'I didn't get Dad's fax until three
weeks after he sent it! I was at a campsite in a remote
part of northern Mexico at the time. Deliveries aren't

exactly reliable in that part of the world. By then the funeral had already been held.' A shadow crossed her face. 'I was *devastated* at missing it.'

As she gulped in a breath, Cam eyed her skeptically. 'But having missed it, you decided there was no rush.' His tone was scathing, his unfair condemnation cutting into her like a knife.

'I *was* rushing—that was the whole trouble! One of our team—an American—offered to drive me across the border to L.A. airport. We were on our way there when the accident happened. I'd leapt out on the way to buy a toy for Emma.'

As Cam's gaze flickered to the giant teddy in her arms she shook her head. 'I bought this yesterday— at L.A. airport. After my stupid fall, I ended up in hospital, having surgery—*micro*surgery—on a badly cut lip. And a couple of days later I was hit by a mysterious bug I must have picked up in Mexico.'

As she paused for breath she noted shakily that Cam's eyes had lost some of their icy scorn. But not much. The very fact that she'd been away for so long—out of reach for so long—obviously weighed against her.

'And it was bad enough to keep you in hospital for another three weeks?'

'Yes!' Indignation flashed in her eyes. 'It completely knocked me out. I had a raging fever…I was delirious for days…and weak as a kitten for days after that. And because of the surgery on my lip, I couldn't even talk to begin with!'

'Well…your surgeons should be commended.' She felt his dark gaze on her mouth. 'There's not a trace

of any scarring. Or bruising. You'd never know you'd
had anything done.'

She frowned. Did he still not believe her?

'They did the repair from inside my mouth—that's
why there's no visible scarring. And the swelling and
bruising have had time to heal, thanks to that horrific
virus. My mouth feels fine. Perfect. *I* feel fine.' She
didn't want him to think she was still weak, and perhaps unable to take care of her niece.

'You still look pale…and very thin…but if you're
feeling fine again, that's splendid.' Taking her bag,
he turned on his heel, freeing her at last of his burning
gaze. 'Come on, Roxy…let's get you settled in.'

CHAPTER THREE

CAM didn't speak as he led her along the main passage to the guest wing. Perhaps, Roxy thought, giving him the benefit of the doubt, he didn't want to risk waking the baby.

Seeing him from behind reminded her—a bittersweet reminder—of the first time she'd ever set eyes on him, as he'd stood at the altar alongside his brother, waiting for Serena and her bridesmaid to join them. Roxy had been the bridesmaid and Cam the best man.

Only their backs had been visible. Cam, the elder brother, was half a head taller than the bridegroom, with shoulders that were considerably wider than those of his equally well-built brother. His glossy dark hair contrasted starkly with Hamish's wiry, gingery mop. At the sight of Hamish's brother, who was to be her partner for the evening, she'd almost overbalanced halfway down the aisle. Her feet, unused to high heels, had rolled over slightly on her long spiky heels.

She'd tried to avoid looking at him after that, but annoyingly, his image had remained. She'd taken a few deep breaths, wondering how she could be so aware of a man after a single, fleeting glance from behind. Normally she had nothing but scorn for roving-eyed, love-'em-and-leave-'em types—the type Cam was rumoured to be.

No woman, Hamish had liked to joke, was safe around Cam. No woman could resist him.

No woman? Roxy had stirred at the challenge.

Cam Raeburn, she'd naively thought at the time, would need more than a pair of powerful shoulders and a head of glossy black hair to hold *her* interest for more than two minutes!

Ha! She'd been like a lamb to the slaughter!

She hadn't come directly face to face with him until they'd moved into the vestry after the ceremony to sign the register.

'Well, I must say you're a surprise, Roxy.' Cam's warm honeyed tones and disarming half smile had threatened to melt her where she stood...until his words had sunk in and her nerve-ends had sprung to full alert.

A surprise? A disappointment, more like! No doubt he'd expected a tall, dark-eyed beauty like Serena. Unless Hamish had warned him that she was the pint-sized, tomboyish, unglamorous sister—and here she was, looking glamorous for once, in a shimmering cornflower blue gown, the colour of her eyes.

She'd gazed up at him coolly, only to feel her eyes waver under the impact of his. His eyes, even darker than her darkeyed sister's, were like shining black opals, filled with fire and light. She'd had to moisten her lips before she could take in the rest of him—the heavy dark brows, the straight nose, the sexy cleft in his chin, the square jaw.

Finally she'd found her voice, tilting her chin to inquire sweetly, 'You were expecting a scruffy little ragamuffin with dirty fingernails and scuffed shoes?'

The half smile had become a real one, a heart-stopping smile of pure charm. She'd wobbled on her high heels.

'On the contrary, Roxy...I was merely expecting someone older—you *are* the older sister, aren't you? Having heard only moments ago how brilliantly clever you are—teaching ancient history at University—I expected, at the very least, to see you wearing blue stockings and bifocals, with your hair tied back in a bun.'

She'd had to smile. He wouldn't be the first man to expect her to look like a fusty academic-simply because she was a qualified archeologist and a lecturer in ancient history. Only Cam hadn't known then, of course, that she was a globetrotting archeologist as well as a history lecturer. Hamish hadn't thought to mention it to him, which wasn't surprising. She'd had no field trips in the past couple of months, and his brother, Cam, had only arrived home that morning from an eightweek overseas business trip.

'The guest wing's through here, Roxy.'

She jumped at the sound of Cam's voice. As he turned to wave her in ahead of him, their eyes met. The impact of his dark gaze was as jolting as ever.

Still the same sexy, charismatic Cam, Roxy thought with a tremulous sigh. But he couldn't affect her any more. She wasn't the naive, trusting Roxy she'd been a year and a half ago.

Not that he'd notice or care. He'd made it clear on at least two previous occasions that he preferred leggy, dark-eyed brunettes to blue-eyed, mop-haired blondes with a tendency to trip over their own feet.

She stepped quickly past him. The guest wing was virtually a self-contained flat, with its own small kitchen, dining area, living room, double bedroom and spacious bathroom. It looked roomy and comfortable, with homey decorative touches that reminded Roxy of her sister. Serena had loved decorating.

'The bed's already made up,' Cam told her as he followed her in.

Roxy, her nerves already taut, tensed further at the mention of 'bed'. She wondered who the bed had been made up *for*. Was it always made up, ready for guests? *Women* guests? Or had Cam rushed in here after her phone-call and made it up specially for her?

Hugging the soft teddy bear, she asked, 'Where's the baby's room from here? I'd like to be near my niece.'

Cam gave her a quick, speculative look, as if he wasn't sure he believed her. 'Mary's taken over the room next door to the nursery. And the master bedroom, where I sleep, is on the other side of Emma's room. Don't worry, Roxy, I'll get up to the baby if she wakes in the night. I normally do anyway.'

Roxy inhaled a carefully drawn breath. She didn't want to start an argument at this point in time, but she had to ask. 'How about moving my niece in here with me, just for the weekend?' Or longer, she thought, if it takes longer. 'It'll be a way of getting to know each other. I'll get up to her during the night if she cries. You can catch up on your sleep.' Her gaze flicked to his face. 'You look as if you need it.'

'Thanks, but it's not necessary.' You're not necessary, he might as well have said. 'I'm managing just fine. Emma already sleeps through the night. She has her last bottle around seven, then sleeps right through until five or six o'clock. She rarely wakes in the night.'

'You don't mind waking up at five to feed her?' Roxy's spirits were beginning to slide. He sounded as if he *enjoyed* looking after the baby.

But for how much longer would his enthusiasm last?

'Not a bit…she's already like a daughter to me,' he said with a firmness that made her forget about being careful.

'My sister wanted *me* to have custody of Emma if anything ever…ever…' Her voice cracked and tears sprang to her eyes. 'I—I still can't believe…' She gulped, a painful lump welling in her throat. Suddenly it was all too much. Grief, jet lag and a build-up of nervous tension swamped her. Burying her face in the teddy bear's soft fur, she burst into tears.

'Roxy…' Cam's arms were round her before she realised what was happening. She couldn't find the strength to fight him as, cradling her in the curve of his shoulder, he gently plucked the teddy bear from her and dropped it onto the bed. She let her head fall onto his chest, helpless tears pouring down her cheeks, splashing onto his shirt.

'It's okay, Roxy…' His low voice vibrated against the damp cheek pressed against his chest. He was stroking her hair with an amazingly gentle hand while he held her close to him with his other. The tender stroking felt so caring, so comforting that she couldn't believe it was Cam Raeburn who was doing it. Weakened by his unexpected sympathy she began to sob in earnest, her breath coming in tremulous gulps, her shoulders heaving, her tearful face still pressed into his T-shirt, soaking the faded fabric.

Cam held her, rocking her as gently as one would rock a baby, until she'd cried out all her bottled-up pain and grief.

Finally she raised her face, furiously blinking away her tears. She didn't want Cam thinking she was falling into a heap and couldn't cope with Serena's baby. 'Sorry, Cam, I...it just caught up with me. Serena...Hamish...the long flight...the lack of sleep. I'm all right now. Truly.'

He drew back and looked down at her, as if to make sure. 'No need to apologise.' He was eyeing her strangely. His voice sounded a bit strange, too, not as cool or as smooth as before. 'It's healthy to cry...even if it—' He clamped his mouth shut and stepped back, letting his hands fall away. His eyes were hidden from her now, and she could sense his withdrawal.

'I'll make you some coffee.' His voice was brusque again, back to normal. 'Come when you're ready, Roxy. I'll be in the kitchen. Just follow the passage.'

He left her to unpack and freshen up. When she joined him in the kitchen a few minutes later, bringing the giant teddy bear with her, he was standing at an island bench, chopping vegetables.

'Stir fry for dinner okay with you?' he asked, waving her to a stool.

'You cook, too?' He was chopping with a practiced air, as if he'd done this chore many times before.

'As a bachelor, you need to be able to cook if you don't want to live on take-away or dine out every night. I've come to enjoy it, even though I have

Philomena to cook for me these days, if I want her to. Do you cook, Roxy?' He glanced up, and she caught the glimmer of doubt in his eyes.

'Give me a camp fire and I'll show you how well I cook,' she answered flippantly, propping the teddy bear on the stool beside her. With a tilt of her small chin she added, 'I might not have your undoubted finesse—I'm no cordon bleu cook—but at least I'll never starve.'

His eyes narrowed under her feisty gaze, and she wished she hadn't reminded him of her roving life-style.

'Mind if we have our coffee here in the kitchen? I can go on with my chopping.' As he poured coffee into two mugs, he asked, 'Did your father give you the details of your sister's will, Roxy?'

Roxy's head jerked up. 'What details?' Custody of Emma, did he mean? According to her father, Serena had made no mention of custody in her will.

'Serena left you a few personal items and some jewellery. I have them in the safe. The Sydney flat that your father bought for you and your sister when he sold your family home and moved to the west coast is now officially yours. It's been virtually yours anyway, I understand, since Serena married Hamish.'

Roxy frowned into her coffee. Was he hoping she'd go back to her Sydney flat and stay there? Or thinking, maybe, that she didn't deserve a city flat of her own, since she was so seldom at home?

'What about…Serena's clothes?' she asked with difficulty, without looking at him. 'Are they still here, waiting to be sorted through?' If Cam was using the master bedroom, he must have either disposed of them or put them aside for her to deal with.

'Blanche went through your sister's things while she and your father were over here for the funeral,' Cam told her, adding almost accusingly, 'You weren't here, Roxy. We hadn't even heard from you.' Then, on a softer note, 'Blanche said that none of Serena's things would fit you anyway—your sister being so much taller. She bundled everything up and sent it off to a charity.'

Roxy shrugged. No doubt Blanche had taken a few things for herself or her married daughter first. Not that she minded. It would be too painful to wear any of Serena's clothes anyway. A piece of jewellery…a few personal items…simply as a memento…that was different.

'Raeburns' Nest now belongs to me.' Cam paused to take a sip of his coffee. 'Everything else—Hamish's share in the pharmacy and any other money or valuables from their joint estate—will be put into trust for their daughter.' He flicked her a look, as if waiting for comment.

Roxy took a deep breath and asked, 'Did Hamish's will mention custody of their daughter?'

As she glanced up, she caught a glint in Cam's eye that filled her with foreboding. He told her, in a level, velvet-soft tone, 'My brother named me as his daughter's guardian. It was his express wish,' he spelt out, 'that I have custody of Emma.'

Roxy's hand jerked, spilling her coffee. 'My sister specifically asked *me* to take care of their daughter if anything ever happened to them!'

Cam's brow shot up. 'I'm sure Hamish wouldn't

have named me, Roxy, without Serena's agreement.
Your sister must have changed her mind. No doubt
Hamish pointed out how impractical it would be to
expect you—a devoted career woman who's away
from Australia for most of the year—to take care of
a young child. He must have convinced her that I'd
be the best one to have custody.'

Roxy sucked in an incensed breath. 'My sister
would never change her mind! Hamish must have
meant that—that he would want you to take care of
Emma *temporarily*…just until I could come back
from wherever I was and take over! Or…or he wanted
you to be her *financial* guardian. That's more like it!
Not her permanent, everyday guardian.'

'I don't think so.'

His calmness infuriated her even more. 'I'll fight
you for custody!' she threatened recklessly.

He laughed. 'You can't possibly want permanent
custody, Roxy. You're never at home. You're always
hightailing off to some remote archeological dig
where you don't even get vital mail when it's sent to
you. And when you do, you trip over things and catch
foreign bugs that keep you away for weeks longer!'

She winced, and jutted her chin. 'I'll give up my
field work. Naturally.'

He shook his head, his smile almost pitying. 'Easy
to say that, Roxy…but not so easy to mean it. Sorry,
sweetheart, but my brother wanted me to have custody of our niece. Your sister gave no written instruc-
tions to suggest that she disagreed.'

'Well, she'd hardly be expecting to die at the age
of twenty-four!' Roxy snapped back. She gulped
down her fury, and after snatching in some breaths of

air said more calmly, 'Surely it's better for a baby
girl to be brought up by a woman—an aunt who can
be a real mother figure to her—than a phil—' She
was about to say 'philandering', but had second
thoughts about hurling insults at this delicate stage.
'Than a bachelor uncle. You surely must know by
now how a baby ties you down.'

Her arguments failed to move him. 'A daughter
should have a father *and* a mother, and I intend to
give Emma both—as soon as I can arrange it.'

Roxy's heart chilled. So her father was right. Cam
was planning to get married again. She felt a sharp
twinge. On Emma's behalf, she told herself frac-
tiously. Poor little soul, having one of Cam's bimbos
thrust onto her.

'Belinda, do you mean?' she asked before she
could stop herself. She clamped her mouth shut. The
thought of the dark-eyed, tennis-playing brunette married to Cam and helping to bring up her baby niece
made her blood boil. Never, she thought. Never!

'Belinda?' Cass looked amused. 'No, it won't be
Belinda. Belinda's gone back to her exhusband. She's
living in Melbourne now.'

Roxy felt an irrational leap of relief, before her
spirits plunged again. *Gone back to her husband…* If
wives could go back to their husbands…

'Is your ex-wife coming back to *you?*' she blurted
out.

Cam laughed. A harsh, scathing laugh, his mouth
twisting. 'Hardly. My wife is happily remarried, and
has a new life far more suited to her than the life I
offered her.'

The mocking black eyes turned cold and flat under
her gaze. Roxy swallowed, moistening her lips with

the tip of her tongue. Did that biting cynicism hide a deep hurt? She felt a wave of sympathy for him.

Until she remembered what was at stake. Her niece. She reached for her coffee, hardening her heart as she gulped it down.

She couldn't afford any weakening towards Cam Raeburn. She had to remain strong enough to fight him.

In the swirling silence a baby began to cry.

CHAPTER FOUR

'LET me go to her,' Roxy offered, jumping up, her hand reaching for the big teddy bear.

But Cam was already on his feet. 'Come with me, by all means, but I think Emma should see a familiar face first up.'

'Oh. Yes…of course.' Although Roxy could see the sense in that, she was only too aware that he was reminding her yet again that she was a virtual stranger to her niece. As she trailed after him to the nursery, she asked, 'You've seen a lot of Emma since she was born?' She was wondering how long Cam had been a familiar face to the baby. Only since his brother's death?

'Enough for her to recognise me with a big smile when I moved in here with her,' he tossed back, and she drew in her lips. It was Cam's fault she hadn't seen more of her infant niece in the past seven months. She'd taken on longer field trips to avoid *him.*

Already she was regretting her long absences abroad. It would have been preferable to risk running into Cam occasionally than to become a virtual stranger to her baby niece.

What if little Emma wanted nothing to do with her? Roxy bit her lip, a rush of nervousness sweeping through her as she followed Cass into the nursery— a light, charmingly decorated room with a window overlooking the lush green cliffs and the deep blue ocean beyond.

Cam lifted the baby from her cot, but her high-pitched wails continued. 'I know, I know, you're wet and you want a clean nappy. And I guess you're ready for your bottle, too.' He seemed surprisingly unperturbed. 'Let's get you out of your wet nappy first, huh?' He glanced round at Roxy. 'I guess she still misses her mother, poor kid. Mary's been a lifesaver. Emma adores her. Mary's been like a grandmother to her.'

Roxy's heart wrenched. She wanted Emma to adore *her,* not an elderly baby-sitter. But she wasn't being fair. If Mary was like a grandmother to Emma, her niece was lucky to have such a caring baby-sitter.

'Can I hold her while you find her a clean nappy?' she begged, her heart going out to the wailing baby as she dropped the teddy bear into the baby's cot and waited expectantly.

'Let's get her changed first.' Cam was already lowering Emma onto a changing table. He had the wet nappy off in a trice, snatching up a clean one from the shelf below. 'Ever changed a baby's nappy?' he asked her with a mocking sidelong glance.

Roxy took a deep breath. 'No,' she admitted. 'But I'm sure if you can master it, so can I.'

'Quite. Watch how I do it, and next time you can have a go.' He fastened the clean nappy with more speed, Roxy noted critically, than finesse. The baby, she thought, definitely needs a woman's touch.

'Thank heaven for disposable nappies,' Cam commented, tickling the baby's tummy. The crying miraculously stopped and the baby began to gurgle, a beautiful smile spreading across her tiny heartshaped face. *'Voilà!'* Cam gave a triumphant grin. 'Feeling better already, aren't you, princess?'

Roxy took a step forward and bent over her baby niece, her eyes misting.

'Oh, she's so beautiful,' she cried involuntarily. The baby had changed so much in the past five months. 'She looks just like—like her mother looked at the same age.' She raised blurred eyes to Cam's face. 'She has Serena's eyes...Serena's lovely smile...Serena's dark hair. Can I hold her now?' she pleaded huskily.

He nodded and stood aside. 'Of course you can.' She caught an odd glint in his eye as she blinked her tears away, but it was gone even before she turned back to the baby. It could have been surprise... doubt...mistrust...she couldn't tell.

'Emma...hullo, sweetheart,' she said gently. 'I'm your aunt Roxy, remember?' With a smile she reached for the baby, bracing herself for a refusal, and renewed wails.

But there were no wails, no refusal. The baby, still smiling her dimpled smile, raised her tiny arms and reached out to her. With a rush of overwhelming love and relief, Roxy gathered her niece in her arms.

As she nursed the baby on her shoulder, stroking her soft hair with tender fingers, overcome by the fragile, sweet-smelling bundle in her arms, she saw Cam watching her. Ready, no doubt, to seize the baby from her if she started crying again. But mercifully she didn't, and Roxy's fears began to slide away. She was over the first hurdle, at least.

'I'll go and get her bottle ready,' said Cam, and he

slipped from the room. Roxy saw the baby's eyes following him, saw her lip wobble, and decided to follow him, cuddling the baby in her arms as she headed for the kitchen.

It was only the second time in Emma's short life that she'd held the baby in her arms, but it felt so different this time—overwhelmingly different. Never had she felt so close to her sister's cherished child, so deeply moved, so filled with love and sadness and joy, all mixed up together. It made her more determined than ever to fill the tragic void her sister's death had left.

But what if Cam wouldn't give up the baby, and insisted on fighting her for custody? What hope would she have of taking him to court and winning? Especially if he had a wife by the time the case came to court. A wife who would care nothing for a baby girl who wasn't even Cam's child—as her own stepmother, Roxy brooded, cared nothing for her.

The baby began to whimper as she spied her bottle, and Roxy murmured softly, 'It's coming, sweetheart, it's coming.'

'She should have had this earlier,' Cam muttered as he popped the bottle into the microwave, 'but she fell asleep before I could give it to her. We're a bit out of our routine today.'

When the bottle was ready he let Roxy feed the baby, suggesting they go into the family room to sit in comfort. Instead of leaving her alone with Emma, he stayed to watch, lowering himself into the armchair opposite. Roxy wondered peevishly if he was still worried about leaving his niece alone with her.

She sighed. It was good that he cared so much for

the baby, but not so good that he thought so little of *her*.

'If you want to go and do something else, feel free,' she invited hopefully. Her suspicion that he didn't trust her with the baby was making her nervous. 'You must have lots of other things you could be doing.' With no Mary for the weekend, and no Philomena to cook and clean up for him...

She gulped as it hit her for the first time. She was here alone with him for the whole weekend. She would be alone overnight with him. And tomorrow night. And maybe she'd still be here next week as well, if Cam hadn't agreed to hand Emma over by then. Assuming he allowed her to stay on.

She began to shake.

The baby made a querulous sound, and Roxy snapped back to earth, cooing softly until Emma settled down again, and resumed her contented sucking on the bottle.

'I'll never keep her from you, Roxy,' Cam promised, his voice bringing her head up with a jerk. 'You can see the baby whenever you want to. Any time,' he said expansively, though his eyes were strangely hooded, she noted. 'Whenever you're at home' he added with a touch of dryness. 'I want her to be close to you, too, Roxy.'

Her blue eyes sparked fire. How generous, she thought caustically. Was he speaking for his new wife, too? Would *she* want a young, single aunt constantly popping into their lives? Or would she want to keep Cam and baby Emma to herself?

Roxy thought of her possessive, mean-streaked stepmother, Blanche, who'd never wanted to share her husband with anybody, not even his own daughters. Would Cam's wife be like Blanche, jealously keeping her husband to herself? Perhaps, in time, even wanting to keep Cam from his niece as well?

Rebellion stirred in Roxy's heart. She couldn't allow it. She wouldn't!

'I'm home for good now,' she announced firmly. 'I'm not going on any more field trips.' She had to make him believe it, and waste no time about it. In the days to come, while she was here at Raeburns' Nest, she would have to make herself indispensable to the baby so that Cam would see that she was the best one to bring up their niece.

It was vital that she took little Emma from him before he plunged into another marriage, purely for the baby's sake. Once he was married, she might find herself shut out of her niece's life altogether, despite what Cam was promising now. His new wife would have no emotional ties with Serena's baby, and a woman who felt nothing for a child could cause lifelong pain and psychological damage to both the child and to everyone who cared for her welfare.

Roxy felt a fierce protective urge towards the helpless baby in her arms. How could any stepmother feel as strongly for Emma as she felt?

She bowed her head over the feeding baby, hiding her eyes from Cam's probing gaze. Even if his new wife welcomed her into their home with open arms…even if the woman proved to be a wonderful mother to Emma…how, Roxy wondered bleakly, could she bear to come back here in the future, knowing that Cam would be here…with another woman?

How could she bear to see him gazing at his wife

the way he'd once, briefly but earth-shatteringly, gazed at her? How could she bear to see him holding his wife the way he'd once held *her?* The way he'd held her again earlier today—even if he'd only been trying to comfort her?

She almost moaned aloud, but managed to turn it into a soft humming sound instead, then into a lilting lullaby—one she remembered her own mother singing when her younger sister, Serena, was a baby. She felt her eyes fluttering as she hummed. Her jet lag was catching up with her. She jerked herself awake as her head nodded forward—unwittingly jerking the baby at the same time.

With a snort of protest, Emma snatched her mouth away from the bottle and began to wave her arms about, her big dark eyes wide and anxious now, as if she were about to cry.

'Getting tired of the baby already, Roxy?' Cam murmured. He was on his feet, plucking the fretful baby from her arms.

'Hi, princess, what's up?' He had a small rubber dog in his hand, Roxy noticed, which he squeezed, making it squeak. Emma smiled and grabbed at it. 'That's better. Well…I guess you've had enough milk. Like a play now?' Lowering the baby onto a colourful blanket on the floor, among her scattered toys, Cam glanced up at an indignant Roxy.

'Taking care of a baby requires a lot of time and tience—and stamina,' he drawled, obviously referring to the way she'd almost nodded off. 'It isn't as exciting as finding an ancient tomb or digging up old bones,' he pointed out dryly. 'It's a relentless routine of feeds, bathing, changing nappies—including smelly, dirty ones—and keeping the baby amused and safe when she's awake.'

Roxy found her voice, if shakily. 'I've just f-flown back from America. It was a long flight and I was so worried about Emma I—I barely slept on the plane!' She was trembling. Even her bottom lip was trembling. She realised she was dangerously close to bursting into tears again. Hysterical tears this time.

Cam would just love that, she thought, pulling herself together with an effort. Hysterical women didn't make capable, calm mothers, he'd be thinking to himself. And he'd be right.

'Maybe you'd better go to bed and sleep it off,' Cam suggested in a marginally gentler tone. 'I can take care of Emma. I'll put her in her stroller and take her for a walk along the cliffs. She loves that. Don't worry about your dinner. I'll leave it for you and you can heat it up in the microwave when you wake up.'

Roxy bit down on her lip, her nerve ends bristling a warning. He was letting her know that she wasn't needed. *I can take care of Emma.*

'They say it's better for your body clock if you keep going until your normal bedtime,' she asserted, drawing herself up and arching her back. 'It was just sitting here for so long that made me drowsy. I'm fine now. Maybe we could have our dinner early?' she suggested in the same breath. 'I'll go to bed straight after that.' Then she wouldn't have to spend the evening alone with Cam. She just didn't feel up to it.

'Whatever you say. You're the guest.'

Just a guest, he might as well have said. She compressed her lips. He obviously didn't expect her to stay at Raeburns' Nest for long…didn't believe that she was serious about giving up her field work to take care of her baby niece. Well, he'd soon find out how wrong he was.

She dropped to her knees beside the baby, who was happily chewing on her rubber dog. 'I'll play with Emma,' she offered, 'while you go and have a shave or something.' It was a gentle reminder that Cam could do with a helping hand himself.

He paused for a moment, then said, 'Right. I will. If Emma kicks up a fuss when I leave the room, you could try taking her for a walk in the garden. That usually works. If it doesn't, you know where to find me. My room's the one next to the nursery—on this side.'

He turned away, thankfully, before he could see the flush that rose to her cheeks. She had no wish to be reminded where his bedroom was!

She slept for twelve solid hours that night, not waking until nine the next morning. She had to force her eyes open against the sunlight streaming into her room. When she squinted at her watch and saw the time she groaned aloud. Cam must have been up for hours already, probably since five this morning, dealing with the baby on his own.

What would he think of her for sleeping in so late? That she didn't care about Emma after all?

She scrambled out of bed and stumbled to the bathroom. She didn't waste time showering, simply splashing her face with water to wake herself up, then dragging on jeans and a T-shirt. She didn't even brush her hair. Not that her short jagged hairstyle looked much different when she did.

She found Cam in the kitchen feeding the baby from a Peter Rabbit bowl. For a second she paused at the doorway, entranced by the sight of this big, tall, very masculine man bending over a baby's highchair, patiently spooning cereal into his niece's open mouth. He was chatting away all the while, giving words of encouragement one second, glowing praise the next, and cracking the odd corny joke—for all the world like any proud *real* father.

She felt an emotional lump swell in her throat. Cam's brother Hamish had been a wonderful father. Now she could see that Cam would make a great father, too.

Would she make as good a mother? She sighed, chewing on her lip. She wouldn't have a home like this to offer Emma, for a start. Or buckets of money, like Cam, for clothes, food, creche fees, schooling...

'Ah, good morning.' As if sensing her presence, Cam glanced round. 'Come in, Roxy, Emma's just finished. Scraped the bowl clean.' He wiped the baby's face clean with a damp cloth. 'Well done, princess!' Little Emma beamed.

Roxy stepped forward, relieved that he'd made no caustic comment about her late appearance. Because he hadn't remarked on it, she did. 'Sorry I slept in—' she began.

He waved a hand. 'I'm glad you did. You're looking much better. You were out on your feet last night.'

'I know. Sorry, I wasn't much company.' She'd almost fallen asleep at the dining-room table, over his excellent dinner, which he'd served up as soon as

they'd put the baby down for the night—with her tiny
arms curled around her new teddy bear.

Roxy could barely even remember what they'd
talked about over the meal. Nothing controver-
sial…she would have remembered that. They'd talked
a little about Hamish and Serena, she recalled with a
tremor, and they'd talked about Emma and her cute
habits and mannerisms, and how she learned to do
something new each day. After dinner Cam had refused her offer of help in the kitchen, pointing to the
automatic dishwasher, and she'd excused herself and
stumbled off to bed.

'You were just fine,' Cam said lightly, turning back
to the baby before she could read what was in his
eyes. 'I slept in, too,' he admitted over his shoulder.
'Emma didn't wake until seven this morning, believe
it or not. I actually had time for a shower and shave
before she woke up.'

Roxy swallowed. She'd noticed. Not only was he
clean-shaven, well scrubbed and smooth-haired, but
he was neatly dressed in a maroon polo shirt, light-
coloured pants, and smart casual shoes. Was it in her
honour? she wondered dubiously. Or was he planning
to go out—leaving her to care for the baby? To test
her dedication, perhaps? To see if she'd be more than
ready to hand the baby back after a few hours alone
with her?

She soon found out. Later in the morning while the
baby was taking a nap and she was hanging out some
washing that she'd insisted on doing for Cam, she
heard the front doorbell ring. When she came back
into the kitchen she heard voices coming from the
family room. Not wanting to intrude, she slipped into

the passage leading to the guest wing, deciding to take a shower and do some tidying up while she waited for Emma to wake up.

A woman's voice wafted through the open door of the family room. 'Let's slip out to a restaurant for lunch, Cam, while you have the chance. This relative of yours can mind the baby for a few hours, surely?'

Roxy's steps faltered. The woman's voice was young and sultry, with a familiar, possessive ring. Was this Cam's future bride?

She spun round. Why was she running away? Why not face the woman, and see what kind of mother Cam intended to inflict on her poor little niece? The sexy-voiced siren sounded more interested in having Cam take her out to Sunday lunch than in spending time with baby Emma. Roxy's blood boiled.

She marched back to the family room. The open door revealed Cam and his female guest sitting side by side on the sofa. The woman, in a tight black dress that showed off her very noticeable curves, was swaying towards Cam, her glossy red lips pouting in invitation, her long dark hair cascading over her slender shoulders…and over Cam's left arm.

Another ravishing brunette! Roxy's blue eyes glinted. Was there no end to Cam's procession of flashy brunettes? Or was this one the last of a long line? The chosen one?

Her thoughts grew blacker than ever.

Cam, she noticed as he glanced up, had some papers on his lap. She felt her heart constrict. Were he and his dark-eyed bimbo in the process of applying for a marriage license? Were these the papers they had to sign?

'Ah, Roxy…come in.' Cam swept the papers aside and jumped up. 'My secretary has just popped in with some documents for me to go through. Since I've had Emma to look after, I've been doing quite a bit of work at home,' he explained, to her secret relief. 'I wanted to give my niece a chance to get used to having me around all the time.'

All the time… Roxy met the challenge in his eyes. He was reminding her that he intended to keep his niece. *I intend to get married as soon as I can,* he'd told her.

Her eyes strayed to the shapely brunette, who was rising with feline grace from the sofa. His *secretary,* he'd said. How convenient for him, she thought, hiding a wave of cynicism behind cool blue eyes.

'Mirella…' Cam turned back to the brunette with a smile that made Roxy reflect bitterly, *Why can't he smile at me like that? Like he did…once, long ago?* 'This is Emma's aunt…Roxy Warren. Roxy's just come back from America…and before that she was at a dig in northern Mexico. She's an archeologist.'

Not, Roxy noted sourly, 'She *was* an archeologist.' Cam still refused to believe that she was serious about giving up her overseas field trips.

'Roxy…' He turned back to her, catching her eye before she had time to hide the hostility in hers. 'This is Mirella Brazzi, who works for me at the Wollongong plant. She—' He stopped, his head swinging round. 'Ah! The baby's awake. Mirella, would you mind if—'

'I'll go to her,' Roxy said quickly, picking up the frail sound a fraction of a second after he did. 'You stay with…Miss Brazzi.' She was normally friendlier, ready to use first names, but she didn't want to get too familiar with Cam's future bride. Assuming Mirella was the one.

'Um…I couldn't help overhearing, Cam,' she confessed before dashing off. 'If you'd like to go out for lunch with Miss Brazzi, please go ahead.' She kept her eyes cool, her face impassive. 'I'll be here for Emma. I'd *like* to spend some time alone with my niece. I'm determined to make up for lost time, now that I'm home for good.'

If his girlfriend knew that the baby's Aunt Roxy was home permanently and prepared to take his niece off their hands—not just for today, but for keeps— she might try to persuade Cam to give the baby up.

Roxy wondered why the idea didn't brighten her as much as it should have.

'Well, thank you, Roxy.' The sultry brunette leapt at the offer. 'I can understand you wanting to have your niece to yourself, now that you're back home. And I'm sure the baby will be happier with an aunt— a mother figure—than a hardworking bachelor uncle, after all. A child *needs* a mother,' she stressed piously. 'And who could be closer than a loving aunt?'

Roxy shot her a grateful look, even as her heart stirred in disgust at the cold-hearted way Cam's girlfriend was dismissing both herself and Cam from the baby's life. Mirella's just like Blanche, she thought bitterly. Another woman's child means nothing to her.

There's no way, she vowed silently, those two will get hold of my niece.

She fled from the room without sparing Cam a glance.

Emma stopped crying the moment she appeared,

holding out her small arms to be picked up. Roxy
smiled and gave her a cuddle, and as the baby gurgled
happily in her arms, Roxy's heart nearly burst with
happiness and relief. Emma likes me, she thought,
and pirouetted around the room with the baby in her
arms.

'Wheee,' she sang as she danced around. Emma
actually laughed aloud.

'She seems to have taken to you,' said a voice from
the doorway.

Roxy wheeled round, almost dropping the baby.
'Cam! I—I thought you were going out to lunch with
your...' she was about to say 'secretary', but recklessly changed it to, 'with your future bride.'

Cam looked startled. Then he laughed. 'Mirella is
not my future bride. And never will be. She's not the
marrying kind. My *secretary*—' he stressed the word
'—can't stand children. Or domesticity. She makes
no secret of it.'

Roxy hid the relief that leapt to her eyes, even as
her lips tightened. Mirella mightn't be interested in
marriage or children, but she was obviously giving
Cam the green light to indulge in a bit of fun and
frolic outside office hours. And she was just his type.
A sexy, dark-eyed brunette.

She heard herself asking on an impulse, 'Was your
ex-wife a blue-eyed blonde, by any chance?'

Maybe Cam steered clear of blondes because his
wife—who'd left him to run off with another man—
had been a blonde. Being betrayed by a treacherous
blue-eyed blond wife might account for his current
obsession with ravishing dark-eyed brunettes.

It could also account for him ditching *her*—another

blue-eyed blonde—at his brother's wedding, and waltzing off with that leggy, dark-eyed brunette.

The memory of that bitter evening simmered in her eyes as she bravely eyeballed him.

Cam stared at her as if she'd gone mad. And she had, a little, she realised with a mixture of frustration and despair. It was so unlike her, bombarding a man with questions about his ex-wife and his lovers. Of course, the family court, she reasoned, would ask far more intimate questions if it came to a custody battle.

'What an extraordinary question,' Cam said finally, tickling the baby under her chin and making her smile again. 'No, Kimberley wasn't a blonde. Why?'

Roxy gulped. 'A redhead?' she hazarded. 'With blue eyes?'

Cam frowned. 'My ex-wife had black hair. And deep brown eyes.'

Roxy blinked, and swallowed. Like Belinda and Mirella and the ravishing brunette at Serena's wedding… She inhaled a shaky breath. So…Cam was still attracted to women who looked like his ex-wife, despite the hurt and humiliation Kimberley must have inflicted on him. Brunettes were the type who turned him on, obviously. Flashy, dark-eyed brunettes.

But he wasn't interested in marrying them. Not since Kimberley. They were only to have fun with and then to discard.

Was his love-'em-and-leave-'em attitude to the brunettes in his life his way of proving to himself— or to his friends—that he didn't care? Or even his way of hitting back at the wife who'd left him for another man? Did he feel, when he used and later discarded the flashy brunettes in his life, that he was using and discarding *her?* His runaway wife? Did he gain some perverse satisfaction from that?

'Are you going to change the baby, or shall I?' Cam said curtly, his tone warning her that the subject of his ex-wife was taboo.

But what about the subject of his *second* wife…his wife-to-be? Roxy wondered as she offered quickly, 'I'll do it.' She put the gurgling baby down on the changing table and set to work, resolving to ask that particular question later. It swirled through her brain for the rest of the day.

If he didn't intend to marry Mirella or any of his other brunettes, who did he intend to marry?

CHAPTER FIVE

HAVING declined Mirella's invitation to lunch, Cam set about making sandwiches, which he packed into a hamper with some fruit and cool drinks, telling Roxy, 'We're having a picnic lunch on the beach. You brought your bathing togs with you, I hope?'

She nodded. She'd packed a swimsuit on the off-chance she might need it, knowing Raeburns' Nest had a pool and was close to the beach.

'Good. Put it on while I feed Emma.' Half an hour later he bundled Roxy and the baby into his station wagon and drove them to Kiama beach.

Never had Roxy enjoyed a picnic lunch so much. It was very pleasant on the beach—warm without being too hot. The baby was well shaded from the sun by a big beach umbrella they'd brought with them. She and Cam took it in turns to play with her on the rug they'd spread out on the sand, giving each of them a chance to go for a jog along the beach or for a swim in the light surf.

They might have been any normal parents, Roxy mused, enjoying a sunny November Sunday on the beach with their child.

It was wonderfully relaxing—until it was her turn to go for a swim. Cam had already taken a dip himself—showing off his splendid body and tan in the process. She was dying for a swim, but it meant removing the shirt she'd kept on until now and showing

51

off the low-cut, high-legged swimsuit she was wearing underneath.

Conscious of Cam's dark eyes on her, she felt her
skin heating—and it had nothing to do with the hot
afternoon sun. For the first time in her life she felt
self-conscious about her body. Which was so silly.
There were dozens of other sun-tanned females on the
beach exposing far more than she was. It wasn't as if
she had anything to be ashamed of or embarrassed
about. Her figure, though slight, was quite neat and
shapely, and her skin was still well-tanned from the
months she'd spent under the hot Mexican sun.

It wasn't shyness so much. It was the way Cam
was looking at her, making no attempt to hide the
appreciative gleam in his eyes. He hasn't changed,
she thought with a sigh, rejecting an unwanted ripple
of pleasure. He's still the roving-eyed bachelor he's
always been, despite his plans to marry. Blondes…
brunettes…whatever's on offer.

She swung sharply away, but she could feel Cam's
eyes burning into her bare back as she scuttled down
the beach towards the incoming waves.

Later, when the baby began to grizzle and rub her
eyes, they packed up and drove back to the house.
Emma was asleep by the time they arrived.

'I've an idea,' Cam said as he brought the station
wagon to a halt in front of the double garage at the
side of the house. 'Let's put her into her stroller in
the shade of those trees by the tennis court, and have
a few hits of tennis while she's having her nap.' He
paused. 'You do play tennis, don't you?'

'I've played a few times at Uni, and through
school, but I'm no Steffi Graf.' And no Belinda, Roxy

mused dryly, remembering the tennis-playing brunette Cam had brought to Emma's christening. Still, she enjoyed a social game, and an energetic set or two of tennis would be preferable to sitting around in the house, risking a confrontation.

She sighed as she stepped out of the car—quietly so as not to wake Emma. The questions she longed to ask Cam were still threatening to spill out, but she didn't want to ask them yet and spoil what had turned into a delightful day—leaving aside the conflicts and emotional undercurrents simmering between them.

Nothing, thankfully, spoilt the rest of that perfect afternoon—other than the turmoil swirling through Roxy's mind, and the skin-tingling reactions of her own body, every time Cam came too close or looked at her in a certain way. His new wife, she thought wistfully, was going to have a wonderful life here at Raeburns' Nest with Cam and little Emma, assuming that she—Roxy—decided not to pursue custody of her niece. She quailed at the agonising thought.

I won't give Emma up, she vowed fiercely. I won't! No woman in this world could love Emma as much as I do, or feel as close to her. Serena wanted *me* to take care of her child, even if her husband believed that his wealthy brother, Cam, would make a better choice—but that was only because Hamish didn't believe I'd be prepared to give up my career to look after my niece.

I'd give up everything for my sister's child, Roxy thought with an intensity that turned her blue eyes to glinting silver. I'd give up my life for her.

Did Cam feel as strongly? Would his new wife?

Cam insisted on cooking dinner again that night,

happily leaving her to attend to the baby's needs and put Emma to bed—without his help this time.

'I wanted you to see as much of your niece as possible while you were here,' he told her over their barbecued steaks and salad, which they were eating in the dining room as before, to be within earshot of Emma if she woke.

He was using the past tense, Roxy noted. *Wanted.* He was reminding her that the weekend was almost over.

She took a long deep breath and said evenly, 'I don't intend to leave here, Cam, without my niece.'

Cam frowned, and she panicked. She didn't want an all-out brawl, if she could help it. 'But there's no rush,' she said quickly. 'I could stay here a bit longer if…if you'll have me. I'm sure Mary won't mind having a bit more time to herself, in her own home, once she hears that I'm here to take care of my niece. You must tell Mary she can still come and see Emma, of course, any time she likes.'

Cam raised an eyebrow. 'You don't have any immediate plans for another field trip? Or any teaching commitments back in Sydney?'

'I told you, Cam—I'm giving up my field work. I've *given* it up,' she corrected. 'And Uni doesn't go back until next March.' This was only November. 'You'll be going to work tomorrow, presumably?' she challenged.

The next day was Monday and if Cam allowed her to stay on here for the week, it occurred to her that she'd have the baby all to herself while he was at work during the day. It would give her a chance to bond even closer with her precious baby niece.

She'd miss having Cam at home, she realised in the same breath—startling herself. She squashed the foolish thought. *You need your head read, Roxy Warren.* She'd only miss him as backup with the baby. As a helpful, supporting father figure.

Anything more… She mentally shook herself. Was she *looking* for more heartache?

'I wasn't planning to go to work tomorrow,' Cam drawled. 'That's why I asked Mirella to bring some work here for me. I might even stay home for the rest of the week, just popping up to the plant from time to time to make sure that everything's going okay. I have an excellent general manager in charge of the plant, and a perfectly capable marketing manager up in Sydney. I can keep in touch with them by phone or e-mail.'

So he *would* be at home…not just tomorrow, but for most of the coming week. She ran a nervous tongue over her lips, her heart picking up an extra beat. Being in such close proximity to Cam was becoming more nerve-racking *emotionally* with each hour, each *minute,* they spent together. How could she survive another few days with him? Another few *nights?*

She wouldn't be able to rush off to her room immediately after dinner tonight—weary as she was after her swim and her few hits of tennis, and dealing with the baby. He'd think she had no stamina at all. She would have to stay around and be sociable, at least for an hour or so.

Unless *he* showed signs that he didn't want to spend any more of his time with *her.* Roxy remembered his future bride. When did he plan to see *her?*

'You said you were planning to get married.' She couldn't hold back the questions any longer. Bursting with the need to know, she let them pour out. 'Doesn't your fiancée care about little Emma? She hasn't been to visit our niece this entire weekend! Or come to see you, either, for that matter. Isn't she missing *you?*' His girlfriend—or fiancée, or whatever she was—hadn't even *called* him, as far as she knew. 'Where *is* this woman you say you're going to marry?'

If *I* were your fiancée, she thought, gulping, I wouldn't be leaving you alone with another woman for a whole weekend.

She caught the odd look on Cam's face, the crooked smile on his lips, and demanded, 'What? Why are you looking like that?' Her deep blue eyes flared, then narrowed. He couldn't have *lied* to her about getting married again, could he, just to get rid of her and keep custody of Emma?

She sucked in a disbelieving breath. 'You *are* getting married, aren't you?' Her tone was accusing, but there was a querulous note underneath—which annoyed her intensely as she heard it.

'You're letting your steak go cold, Roxy,' Cam said coolly. 'Eat up, and I'll tell you all.'

'I've had enough.' What remained of her steak and salad looked decidedly unappetising at that particular moment. She didn't want to hear 'all'. But she'd asked, and she'd have to listen. With a sigh she reached for her barely touched glass of wine, and sat back waiting, hardly breathing, her heart thudding in her chest.

'I do intend to get married,' Cam said steadily, 'for

Emma's sake.' He toyed with the stem of his glass. 'But I haven't as yet…asked anyone. *Found* anyone…suitable,' he admitted in the same even tone.

As Roxy's fingers almost cracked the stem of her own glass, he went on in the same level monotone. 'The woman I marry will have to be totally committed to my niece. Devoted to her. Naturally she and I will have to be reasonably compatible as well, physically and philosophically—sharing similar values and principles—though love,' he added with a cynical quirk of his lips, 'needn't necessarily come into it.'

Roxy's breath whistled out through her teeth. There was no emotion in his voice at all. He might have been talking about a job applicant, she thought, eyeing him over the rim of her glass.

Yet she felt a weight slipping from her. Even a vague flicker of hope. He had no bride in mind as yet. No suitable candidate as yet. That put them back on an equal footing. A bachelor uncle and a single aunt, both wanting custody of their niece.

It also raised other possibilities that she thrust vehemently to the back of her mind.

'Look,' Cam said in a milder tone, 'let's just see how we both go over the next few days. You say you're prepared to give up your field work to bring Emma up yourself—'

'I am!' Roxy didn't hesitate. 'And it doesn't matter how many more days I stay here, Cam, I won't change my mind. I intend to bring Emma up as my own daughter. Just as my sister would have wanted me to.'

His brow shot up. 'As a single mother, Roxy? In a

tiny city flat, on a lecturer's wage? Leaving your child in a creche with strangers while you're working?'

Roxy flushed, inwardly wincing. He was comparing her life to his. Comparing his home and his wealth to hers. 'Plenty of single mothers do it perfectly successfully. We'll manage. It's love that a child needs most of all. Love and a feeling of security.'

'It's parents who are around all the time that a child needs most of all,' Cam said, his tone turning harsh. 'You'll have to work long hours to support her. What if things get tough for you financially, Roxy, or you start to miss your exciting overseas field trips and decide to take another trip now and then, leaving your niece for weeks or months at a time? I don't want Emma suffering any more hurt or anxiety unnecessarily, and feeling abandoned all over again. She's already lost the two people closest to her.'

'I won't be abandoning her! I wouldn't do that to her! *Ever.*' Why didn't he believe her? Why was he being so hard on her? What did it take to convince him? 'You're more likely to leave her than I am. You have a demanding business to run. And you'll be wanting to take business trips interstate or overseas...'

'That's why I need a wife,' Cam said calmly. 'Emma needs two parents who love her equally, and it seems to me,' he said slowly, 'that there's only one solution.'

Roxy held her breath.

'If you and I were to marry, Roxy, it would solve both our dilemmas,' Cam said coolly, and sat back in his chair, his arms folded across his chest. He might have been a hard-headed executive proposing a business merger or closing a satisfactory deal. As a marriage proposal, it lacked a lot.

Except maybe a glimmer of sense.

That was Roxy's initial reaction, until the reality hit her like a thunderbolt. Cam Raeburn was asking her to marry him! Roving-eyed, brunette-obsessed Cam, with one failed marriage behind him already, was now coldly proposing another, purely for the sake of their niece! Feelings, emotions, would play no part in this 'suitable' marriage he was proposing. *Love needn't necessarily come into it,* he'd said. It would be a purely practical arrangement, to give Emma a secure home and a loving family, and to avoid an ugly, potentially damaging custody battle.

She looked down at the unfinished meal in front of her without even seeing it. Anything to avoid looking at Cam. Feeling the way she did about him—yet hating the feeling, knowing he didn't feel anything for *her,* and that, as his wife, she would never be able to trust him out of her sight—how could she plunge into such a cold-hearted, loveless arrangement, and expect it to work? Even for her niece's sake, the price would be too high!

Instantly she felt a rush of shame. No price would be too high when it came to her sister's baby. She'd do anything—*anything*—to give back to her niece the love and security that poor little Emma had lost on the death of her parents. Cam mightn't love her, but they got on well enough to make it work, if she didn't expect too much. This weekend had been close to idyllic…if she could blot out the alluring Mirella's appearance.

Could she? She swallowed. Cam might have

knocked back his sexy secretary's invitation to lunch today, but once he was back at work and out of her sight, he'd be able to lunch with Mirella whenever he wished, and she'd be none the wiser.

She gave a deep quivering sigh.

'Panicking already, Roxy? Getting cold feet at the thought of losing your independence and putting someone else ahead of your precious career?'

Her eyes snapped to his, and she could tell, by the mocking glint in his eye, that he'd been noting her changing expressions, her doubts, her apprehension. But it wasn't the thought of giving up her independence or her field trips that was making her so unsure, it was her uncertainty about Cam as a caring, trustworthy husband!

If she hadn't felt anything for him—if she'd been totally indifferent to him as a man—she might have been able to face up to a philandering husband and a cold-hearted marriage of convenience, knowing that he could do nothing to hurt her. But she did feel something for him—there was no point denying it, hard as she might try. She *did.* Too much, she realised painfully. She knew that he *could* hurt her…badly.

She cleared her throat. 'Marriage…to me…means more than just getting together for a beloved child's sake,' she forced out. 'It means commitment and loyalty and—' She hesitated, biting her lip. It was pointless bringing feelings into it. He'd already discounted feelings.

'As Emma gets older,' she said instead, 'she'll sense if we're not…if we don't…' She didn't want Cam to think she was asking for an avowal of love, so she finished in a rush. 'If we don't care for each other. If there's no—no warmth…no real closeness between her parents.'

She flicked a wary look across the table at him. Was he even listening? He was pushing back his chair, rising to his feet, stepping away. She thought for a second that he was going to grab the dinner plates and head back to the kitchen, but instead he moved around behind her. Next moment his hands were on her shoulders, drawing her to her feet, swinging her round to face him.

CHAPTER SIX

As HER lips parted in startled surprise, he dragged her into his arms, dipped his head and kissed her. It was a deep, demanding kiss. Demanding a response from her. A kiss with all the power and passion and scorching heat of a...of a genuine lover, she thought dazedly.

And she *was* responding. She could feel every pulse and nerveend in her body leaping to life, every bone dissolving, every sense reeling. The heat of his lips was drawing fire from her own, quickening the breath in her throat and sending fiery blood pounding through her veins. Her brain had ceased to function and her senses were driving her...driving her wild.

As his tongue slid between her lips, a convulsive need shook her from deep within. Breathing in heavy gasps, she met his demand, thrusting and parrying with her own tongue, clinging to him as if she'd never let him go, knowing in a dim part of her brain that she didn't want to let him go, that whatever he wanted, she would go along with.

She gasped for air as Cam finally raised his head. He gave a low chuckle as he watched her, a satisfied gleam in his eyes. 'I don't think you need to worry about us not caring enough for each other, Roxy.' His voice, usually so velvety smooth, sounded thick and unnatural, as if he'd been as aroused as she. 'You can't deny there's a powerful chemistry between us.'

Chemistry... Drawing on all her reserves of strength, she took a step back, eyeing him speculatively through her lashes. So he did feel *something*. Not love, of course. Not even tenderness. Nothing so sentimental. But he *was* attracted to her...physically.

He was attracted to a lot of women *physically*. Sexy brunettes in particular. Her lip wobbled. He'd dumped her at Serena's wedding to chase after one of his flashy brunettes. Obviously brunettes radiated more chemistry than pintsized, gaminfaced blondes. But she radiated enough, he'd just taken pains to show her, to give their marriage a good chance.

'Will you marry me, Roxy?' This time the proposal held more warmth. A gentle, seductive warmth. His hands were still curled round her arms, though their bodies were no longer touching. If they had been she wouldn't have been able to think at all. It was bad enough feeling the warmth of his fingers seeping into her skin.

'I'm sure we can make it work, Roxy...if you're seriously prepared to give up your career to live here at Raeburns' Nest with Emma and me and become a fulltime mother to our niece. It will mean giving up your teaching job in Sydney as well—at least until Emma starts school.'

As Roxy took a deep breath, he stressed, 'I want Emma to have love and security. *Constant* love and security. Which means a safe, secure home and loving, hands-on parents. I don't mind you doing some more teaching eventually, Roxy, but disappearing for months at a time on remote field trips is out. Even school-age children need a mother around, at least for part of the day.'

'I agree with you,' Roxy assured him. She stifled a sigh. He still wasn't sure of her. He still couldn't believe that she was serious about giving up the field work she'd always loved...the career she'd always put first.

Well, *she* was still unsure of *him.* Sexual chemistry wasn't love. It wasn't affection. All he felt for her was a powerful animal lust. A purely physical attraction, that didn't affect him at a deeper, more tender level. Would it be enough to stop him straying into the arms of another ravishing brunette when the temptation—and the opportunity—arose? Would she mind very much if he did?

A deep quiver shook through her. Oh, Roxy, you poor fool, she lamented, wishing that pure lust was all she felt for *him.* It would make this momentous step so much easier. But what she felt for Cam—she had to face it—went deeper than sexual chemistry, deeper than a passing infatuation. She'd had fleeting passions and lustful feelings before and they'd never felt like this...never shaken her like this. She'd never felt as strongly for any man before in her life. She doubted if she ever would again.

Could she still go ahead with it? Would she be doing the right thing, agreeing to a loveless, one-sided marriage? She took another step back, wanting to put more space between them, and Cam let his hands slide from her arms and drop to his sides.

'You're quite sure you'll be able to give up your archeological field work, Roxy?' he pressed, and she gathered her strength and forced her gaze back to his. He was frowning, his eyes searching her face, as if trying to read her innermost mind. He thought she was hesitating because of her career. He had no idea it was because she'd lost her head over *him* and was afraid of getting badly hurt!

Badly hurt? With a wrench of her heart she thought of her poor motherless niece, who'd suffered more hurt than anyone could ever imagine. Emma was the one who needed love and caring the most, and if she married Cam, their niece would have two loving parents again—the two people who loved her most in the world.

Roxy jerked up her chin and pushed her own foolish yearnings aside.

'Quite sure,' she said, her blue eyes perfectly clear now, showing no doubt at all.

'Then you'll marry me?' A tiny flame flickered deep in the black depths. Relief, she guessed, that he'd averted a distressing custody battle.

She eyed him steadily, not hesitating this time, thinking only of her baby niece. 'If it's going to be the best thing for Emma, then yes, I'll marry you.'

There was a pause before he spoke again. 'I hope it will be the best thing for us, too, Roxy.' He reached out a hand, brushing her soft cheek with his fingers.

She jumped, almost leaping back at his touch. Now that she'd accepted his proposal, did he think he had the green light to race her off to his bed? She felt a flare of panic. She wasn't ready for that yet…to face up to sex without romance…without love… 'Maybe we could discuss the practical details of our—our arrangement while we're clearing up in the kitchen,' she breathed, neatly sidestepping him and starting to gather up the plates, hoping the mention of practical details would dampen any lustful urges.

Unfortunately her practical suggestion had come out in a jerky, breathless, embarrassingly *im*practical rush.

'You go ahead,' Cam said with a quirk of his lip- as if finding her nervous rebuff amusing. 'I'll be with you in a minute. I want to make a couple of phone calls.'

Her eyes followed him uncertainly as he strode from the dining room. Was he deliberately removing himself from her, now that he had Emma's future settled? Maybe he needed to take a breather himself, after the momentous decision he'd just reached.

Who would he be calling at this hour on a Sunday night?

A woman?

She groaned, exasperated with herself. Was she for-ever going to have lurid visions of Cam's other women haunting her?

She had the kitchen spotless by the time he came back. When he ambled in, looking breathtakingly sexy in his tight jeans and woven shirt, his towering height and athletic frame seemed to dwarf everything else in the room. He was looking pleased with him-self, she thought, and a bit mysterious. He had a small black box in his hand, she noticed.

'Let's go into the family room,' he suggested, paus-ing inside the doorway. 'I've something for you, Roxy. And something to tell you.'

She assumed that the box in his hand—a jewel box?—must be the 'something for you'. But the 'something to tell you' sounded a bit ominous.

She walked stiffly ahead of him to the family room, and chose an armchair to sit on rather than the sofa.

She could think better when she wasn't within touching distance of him.

She eyed the small box in his hand. *Something for you…and something to tell you…* Was he about to give her a piece of jewellery to seal their engagement, and then—having softened her up—tell her that he'd be wanting a certain amount of freedom in their marriage?

Her mouth went dry. Would he be that blatant? After she'd already told him she believed in commitment and loyalty in a marriage? No… She hissed her breath out through her teeth. If he intended to play around he'd be more discreet about it, more devious. He'd try to keep the little wife happy at home—he'd already demonstrated just how happy he could make her—before sneaking off in search of more exciting challenges elsewhere.

Her mouth sagged open as Cam dropped down on one knee in front of her.

'What on earth are you—'

'I'm making it official,' he said, and opened the small box in his hand. It held a delicate gold ring with a single red stone, unadorned except for the tiny gold claws holding it in place. Though small and unpretentious, the deep red stone was exquisitely beautiful. Roxy knew, without knowing anything about valuable jewellery, that this was a genuine ruby.

As Cam took her hand and slipped it onto her third finger—a perfect fit!—he murmured, 'It was my grandmother's wedding ring. I thought you might like it as an engagement ring…at least until we have a chance to buy you a ring of your own choice.'

'Cam, it's beautiful.' She felt moved that he'd offered her something that must mean so much to him. 'I couldn't have chosen anything more beautiful, or anything I'd like more.' She glanced up at him, feeling suddenly hot-cheeked and flustered. But of course, he wasn't giving it to her to keep…it was just until he bought her a ring of her own, he'd said.

'I—I'll be proud to wear it until…until…' She gulped in a rallying breath and asked in a rush, 'Cam, may I wear it until our—our wedding day? Once I have a wedding ring I won't need an engagement ring. There are such beautiful wedding rings these days, I won't need both.'

She caught a glint of surprise in his eyes. He gave her a long look, as if wanting to check that she meant it. 'If you like it, Roxy, it's yours,' he said. 'We won't need to look for another engagement ring if you'd like to keep this one. I just thought you might prefer—'

'Oh, no…this is just perfect. It's beautiful. Cam, are you sure? You said—'

'I didn't think you'd *want* to keep it. My first wife didn't want it. She didn't like it at all. It wasn't big enough, or modern enough, or sparkling enough. She wanted diamonds. Glitz. Glamour. I assumed all women did.'

Roxy dropped her gaze. Did he prefer his women to be glamorous and glitzy? He'd certainly chosen glamorous females in the past, when it had been a matter of choice. In her case, he hadn't had much choice.

'Not all women,' she muttered. 'If it's glitz and glamour you want, Cam, maybe we'd better think twice about this marriage. I'm just me. No frills. No glitzy trappings. What you see is what you get.' *A *messy-haired, unsophisticated tomboy with simple tastes and plain, down-to-earth needs.*

'What I see,' Cam said with a slow upward curve of his lips that brought extra crinkles to his cheeks, 'is fine with me.' He hauled himself to his feet—rather abruptly, she thought, as if trying to avoid closer scrutiny. She felt her heart dip a little. 'How about some coffee?' he suggested. 'No, you stay there, I'll get it. Over our coffee we'll start making plans.'

Plans. To spend the rest of their lives together. To spend the rest of *her* life with a man who didn't love her. Roxy hauled in a deep breath, trying to stifle a flare of panic. She would just have to *make* him love her.

She felt an hysterical giggle rising in her throat. How in the world did you make a man love you? Especially when he was a cynical, roving-eyed divorcee who'd shown no interest in marrying again until it had been forced on him.

Making a man like Cam love you—making him love you enough to give up his philandering ways and devote himself solely to one woman—would be a challenge and a half.

CHAPTER SEVEN

'NEXT *month?*' Roxy stared at Cam over the rim of her coffee mug. 'As soon as that?'

Cam had spent the past twenty minutes outlining the plans he had in mind, leaving her head reeling.

'It'll give you four weeks to get used to the idea of marrying me...won't that be enough?' His eyes were smiling, but his expression was inscrutable, impossible to read. 'Or looking at it another way: it gives you four weeks to back out. I want you to be quite sure this is what you want, Roxy—not just what you think is right for Emma. If I'm going to get married again, I want to feel confident that it's going to last.'

'I won't change my mind,' she assured him, though her heart fluttered at the thought of what lay ahead. She could be happy being married to Cam, she thought resolutely. She wanted it to be a happy marriage...for Emma's sake, even more than her own. Serena and Hamish's marriage had been so blissfully happy, until that freak storm had cut it tragically short. Their daughter deserved whatever happiness she and Cam could provide.

'And you're happy to have a marriage celebrant conduct the ceremony here at Raeburns' Nest...with just Mary and Philomena as witnesses?'

'Perfectly happy.' They'd already agreed that under the circumstances the ceremony should be as simple and lowkey as possible. Roxy hadn't even wanted her father and stepmother to come, preferring, she'd told Cam, to let them know about the wedding when it was a *fait accomplit*.

'My father's pretty frail these days,' she'd reminded him, 'and it's such a long way for them to come at their age, in their state of health. And it would be too emotional for Dad. I'd rather just get married quietly, and let everyone know later.'

Cam hadn't argued. He'd seemed almost relieved, Roxy thought, swallowing. Of course, he'd been through all the fuss and fanfare of a wedding before, with his first wife, Kimberley—a woman he'd loved. He wouldn't want to go through it all again with a woman he was only marrying for the sake of his niece.

Not having a proper wedding or being a proper bride wouldn't worry her. Not for a minute. She hated fuss, hated dressing up, hated being the focus of attention.

'She's coming tomorrow morning to meet us.' Cam's voice cut through her thoughts.

'She?' Roxy blinked, trying to pick up the thread of the conversation.

'The marriage celebrant. The person I rang earlier, right after I called Mary to tell her you'll be here to look after Emma from now on. The celebrant's name is Grace Browne and she'll be bringing some papers for us to sign.'

'Oh.' The marriage celebrant was a *woman.* If she's a ravishing brunette, Roxy thought with a whimsical curve of her lip, I'll push her over the cliff.

'She sounded a pleasant, sensible lady,' Cam said

reassuringly. 'Warm, rich voice, not too jokey. I bet she sings in a choir. She's—' He broke off, listening for a second. 'Emma's crying! Why would she be crying at this hour?' He frowned. 'She's been sleeping through the night without a murmur. I hope she's not sick.'

Roxy dumped her coffee mug and sprang to her feet. 'Maybe she needs her nappy changed. Or she's too hot. I'll go to her,' she offered.

'I'll come, too.' Cam sounded as concerned as any father, Roxy thought as she darted from the room. And she, she had to admit, felt as anxious as any new mother.

Using the passage lights to guide her, she ran into the nursery to Emma's cot. The baby was screaming in earnest by now. As Roxy picked her up Cam muttered from behind, 'She's kicked off her covers... maybe she's cold.'

He was standing at her shoulder, his head so close to hers that Roxy could feel his breath on her cheek. But it was the baby in her arms he was interested in, not her.

'She feels as warm as toast,' she answered over the baby's wails. 'Switch on the lamp,' she ordered, and breathed a little more freely as he stepped away. 'Look at her cheeks—they're awfully red,' she said worriedly. She felt the baby's brow with the back of her hand. 'She feels quite hot, but I don't think she has a fever. She's not burning hot.'

'How do her eyes look?' Cam's face almost touched hers as he peered into the baby's tear-filled eyes. 'Mary says when a baby has a temperature they'll be glazed and dull.'

'They *look* okay,' Roxy said, though it was hard to tell through the tears. She nestled the baby in the hollow of her shoulder, gently rubbing her back. 'I'll change her nappy and try putting her down again. I think she might be teething. Red cheeks are a sign, I remember Serena telling me once.'

Cam looked unsure. 'Do you think I should call the doctor? Or ring Mary for advice?'

'I don't think we need to call a doctor yet…' Roxy was already lowering the fretful baby onto the changing table. 'And I don't want to ring Mary at this time of night, unless it's an emergency. Maybe we could call her in the morning and ask her to pop over then and take a look at Emma.'

Cam nodded. 'I want to see Mary anyway, to ask about Emma's meals. With babies this age you're introducing new foods all the time.'

As Roxy changed the baby's nappy, she whispered, 'Let's try putting her back to bed for now and see how she goes.' She picked up the still whimpering baby and gave her another cuddle. Then she signalled to Cam to switch off the lamp and leave the room, before carefully lowering the baby back in her cot.

It took her a few minutes to settle Emma down. Leaning over the side of the cot, she stroked the baby's cheek until the soft whimpers eventually died down. Finally, to Roxy's relief, they stopped altogether and the baby's flickering eyes closed—and stayed closed. When her breathing became steady and even, Roxy carefully withdrew her hand and crept from the room.

Cam was waiting in the passage. 'Good work,' he

whispered. 'You're a natural, Roxy. You're going to make a wonderful mother.'

It warmed her that he thought so. One day, perhaps, he'd think her a wonderful wife as well. A wife worthy of loving, the way he'd loved his first wife.

Did he still love Kimberley? she wondered as she paused in the passage, unsure whether to go back to the family room and finish her coffee or go to bed.

A memory quivered through her…a teasing remark that Cam's brother Hamish had made, as they'd danced together at his wedding.

'What have you done to my brother, Roxy?'

When she'd asked what he meant, Hamish had given a knowing smile and said, 'There's a new light in his eye. I haven't seen him so alive since the day he married Kimberley. Not that the spark I saw then lasted for long. His wife walked out on him within months. Ran off with another man.'

Roxy's lips tightened at the memory. The spark hadn't lasted long between Cam and herself, either. It hadn't even lasted the night! One minute he was kissing her passionately, the next he was whisking her back to the bridal table, leaving her with her parents while he waltzed off.

Why *had* his wife run off with another man? Because Cam had grown bored with one woman and sought distractions elsewhere, driving his disgruntled wife into another man's arms?

Roxy blew out a sigh. It was time to deal with more practical matters.

'Cam, I'd like to move out of the guest wing and sleep closer to Emma,' she said firmly, and felt a prickle of heat in her cheeks, knowing that the closest rooms to the nursery were Mary's room—and the master bedroom, where Cam slept. She hastened on. 'Now that Mary's no longer living in, maybe I could move into her room.'

'Mmm…no, you can't do that.' Cam drew her away from the nursery door. 'Mary still has some of her things in there. And besides, we might want her to baby-sit for us, and have her stay here overnight. We're bound to want to spend a night in Sydney now and then, or have dinner out somewhere along the coast, and it's easier for Mary if she can sleep here.'

He was speaking as if they were married already…as if they were going to be doing things together other than looking after the baby. Roxy felt a tremor ripple through her at the images that leapt into her mind. Images of a real marriage…of being a real husband and wife.

'Well, if I can't move into Mary's room, isn't there a—*what are you doing?*' she yelped, realising that Cam was steering her into the master bedroom next door. 'Why are we coming in here?' Her voice had gone up a decibel, turning into a pathetic squeak.

She filled her lungs with a quick gulp of air. 'Don't tell me,' she quipped, 'that you want me to turn down your bed for you, now that I've promised to marry you?'

The quip died on her lips as she silently cursed herself for bringing his attention to the bed. Not that either of them could very well avoid it…it took up most of the room. A huge bed, king-size, with a carved cedar bed head and a cosy-looking duvet with plump pillows.

'It's mighty comfortable,' Cam told her, his gaze

following hers. 'And big enough for at least four people. Two people could get lost in it, and never know there's anyone else in the bed. You're welcome to share it, Roxy. You'll be sharing it anyway in a month's time.'

The hairs rose on the back of Roxy's neck. My, but he was a fast worker! But she'd seen that before, at Serena's wedding. The way he'd kissed *her* one minute—and was all over that leggy brunette the next.

'I'm an old-fashioned girl,' she said with a shrug, the huskiness in her voice betraying her. 'I believe in waiting until my wedding night...doubly so in circumstances like ours.' A marriage of convenience. That was all it was going to be. He'd given her a month to get used to the idea. *Or to change her mind.*

What if she shared his bed now, and then changed her mind about marrying him—or he changed his—before the wedding? She'd just be another notch on his scoreboard, another easy conquest for him to chalk up. And she was damned if she was going to be added to his undoubtedly lengthy list.

'I consider an engagement a courtship—a chance for a couple to get to know each other—not an open license,' she said tartly, and stifled a sigh. Things could have been so different if they'd both loved each other. If *he'd* loved *her,* she corrected painfully. She would gladly have shared his huge bed under those fairytale conditions. The very thought of it stirred sensations she didn't even want to think about.

Cam bowed, rather mockingly. 'Courtship it is, then,' he agreed. 'You can still have the bed, my sweet. I'll take the couch in there...' He waved a hand to an alcove off the bedroom, visible through an archway. 'My private refuge,' he drawled. '*Our* private refuge,' he amended.

Her cheeks burned. Her eyes were riveted to the huge king-size bed. He was inviting her to sleep *there?* To have it all to herself, while he slept a few feet away on a couch?

'Don't be silly, you can't sleep on a couch.' She let her gaze run down his long athletic frame, pricklingly aware of the powerful muscles, the vibrant sexuality, the sexy bulge under his jeans. 'Isn't there another bedroom?' she squeaked. She hadn't seen all the rooms yet, she realised.

'Oh, yes, there are a couple of other bedrooms at the far end of the house, and in the guest wing, of course. But no others here, near the nursery.'

'Then I'll sleep in Mary's room, and move out whenever she comes to stay the night,' Roxy decided querulously. 'I'll go and make up the bed now.' She was ready to scurry off, but Cam's hand caught her arm.

'There's no need to share a room with Mary. Why not use the den opposite the nursery? It's small, admittedly, and has no view, but it's next door to the main bathroom, and the couch in there converts into a bed. It'll do as a temporary measure as you insist on sleeping elsewhere than in here until our wedding night.' His eyes danced wickedly, the invitation in them blatantly obvious.

She tossed her head, making sure she didn't glance at the big bed this time. 'Why didn't you tell me the den has a sofa bed?' she snapped, shaking off his hand, hotly aware of a stifling sensation in her throat.

It annoyed her that a mere touch could affect her
to such a piteous extent.

'I thought it was worth a try.' His eyes were teasing. 'What eager, red-blooded fiancé *wouldn't* give it
a try?'

She made a pathetic attempt at a careless laugh.
'You'll have to *earn* a place in my bed,' she warned
recklessly. 'I don't sleep with just anybody. Only men
I care about…and who care about me.' Her voice
wobbled a bit.

'You have a month,' she said briskly, 'to show me
that you can care enough about me to make this marriage work. And I'm not talking about sex,' she was
quick to add, 'or—or love. Just…caring,' she finished
lamely. 'Caring and…loyalty. F-fidelity,' she spelt
out, to make it quite clear what she meant.

'Sounds fine to me,' Cam said coolly, and she wondered if he was being too cool—too ready to agree—
without really meaning a word of it. 'And *you* have
a month,' he tossed back at her, 'to prove to me that
you won't get itchy feet and want to go off on another
field trip…and then another…and another…'

He was worried about his niece, Roxy thought, not
about her…being apart from her.

'I won't,' she said flatly. 'Archeology's a single
person's career, not one for a wife and the mother of
a young child. I want to be here for my niece,' she
stressed. And for my husband, she added silently, but
that wasn't what they were discussing.

'And what about *our* children?' Cam asked quietly.
'You'll agree to have more children…with me?'

She would want nothing more. But not until she
knew that she could trust him to be faithful, to be a

real husband to her. She believed in two people being totally committed to each other in a marriage—totally loyal to each other. Fidelity mightn't mean much to some women—to women who had affairs themselves, or who didn't love their husbands the way—

She felt a suffocating tightness claw at her throat. Was it really love she felt for Cam? Could you love someone you were so unsure of? After so little time together?

Cam was frowning, she realised with a twinge of unease. He thought she was hesitating over having his children. She stifled a groan. 'If we do get married,' she said carefully, feeling warmth rising to her cheeks, 'of course I'd want more children. I'd want Emma to have a brother or sister—or both. Of course I would.'

Cam nodded, but his eyes had flattened under her gaze. He was still as unsure of her, she thought with a sigh, as she was of him.

'I'd better start moving my things into the den,' she said, swinging round, away from him. 'Goodnight, Cam.'

'Goodnight, Roxy.'

They might have been two wary-eyed strangers, politely taking their leave of each other.

And we are virtual strangers, she thought as she fled to the guest wing to fetch her things. Strangers who barely know each other at all.

Strangers who are about to get married. For life.

The wedding date was set for the week before Christmas. 'It's a good time for me to take a couple of months off,' Cam commented. They might have been business partners arranging a necessary break together for the good of the business. Perhaps that was how he saw his marriage…purely as a business partnership.

'You can choose where we go for our honeymoon, Roxy, as long as it's a suitable place to take an eight-month-old baby—as she'll be then.'

Not to a hot, dusty archeological site, he meant.

'December's not the best month to go up north—or to Europe,' Cam went on musingly. 'It'll be either too hot in the tropics or too cold in Europe. Same with North America.'

He didn't mention Mexico or South America, she noticed—her old stamping ground. No, he wouldn't want her growing nostalgic or getting itchy feet again.

Or was he thinking of the baby? Trying to find the most suitable place for *her*?

'We could go to New Zealand…the south island, perhaps?' Cam suggested. 'It wouldn't be so hard on Emma. We could hire a car and tour around. Ever been to New Zealand, Roxy?'

'Only the north island. Auckland. And only passing through.' On her way to South America and Mexico. But she mustn't think about her old life. She had a new life now, a life that could be even more fulfilling if only… She blinked the thought away.

'That sounds lovely,' she said, trying to sound enthusiastic, but unable to hide a wistful note in her voice. She'd feel a lot more enthusiastic if she knew that her future husband loved her and didn't simply want a caring a mother for his niece and a convenient female in his bed.

She felt Cam's eyes on her. Was he wishing things

could be better, too? Wishing she were a striking, dark-eyed brunette with long raven hair and legs up to her armpits instead of a diminutive, mussy-haired blonde?

Wishing, perhaps, that his brother, Hamish, had married the older sister rather than the younger one, leaving the ravishing, raven-haired Serena for him? Roxy swallowed. Hamish had remarked to her once that he was glad that Serena had met him first, before his dashing brother had come on the scene.

Would Serena have been happy with Cam? She doubted it. Her sister would have been too gentle and sensitive for a dynamo like Cam Raeburn. She would have let him walk all over her and been heartbroken if he'd strayed. As he probably would have. From what she'd seen of him so far, Cam preferred more lively, flamboyant females. He would have tired of gentle Serena after a time and ended up making her life miserable.

Would he grow bored with her, too?

With Mary calling in the next morning and the celebrant arriving in the afternoon and agreeing to stay for dinner, Monday flew by in a whirl—which was probably a good thing. Roxy had no time to think.

From Tuesday on Cam began to spend a few hours each day at his plant at Wollongong, half an hour away. Most days he was home for lunch. On the days he wasn't, Roxy tried not to think about the female colleague he might be having lunch with.

One sunny afternoon, as she was gathering dry washing from the clothesline, she noted a pink smudge on the collar of the shirt Cam had worn yesterday.

A sick feeling coiled through her. Lipstick!

Had Cam taken his sexy secretary out to lunch the day before? Was he already being unfaithful to his future bride, despite his vow that he was genuinely committed to their coming marriage? Or was she just being paranoid?

It was *pink* lipstick. Did Mirella wear pink lipstick? Roxy had only seen Cam's secretary that once, and her lipstick had been bright red. But a woman could change her lipstick with every outfit she wore.

She thought of confronting Cam with the shirt and rejected the idea. If he denied it was lipstick, it would be too humiliating for words. If he admitted it... She shuddered. It would mean she'd have to decide whether to marry a man who was openly unfaithful to her...or have the painful choice of either fighting Cam for custody of her niece or giving up all claim to Emma and removing herself from their lives.

She couldn't risk losing Emma!

With a heavy hearts he headed for the laundry to scrub the collar clean.

That evening, as she was standing at the kitchen sink after dinner, washing the baby's bottles as if her life depended on it, Cam came up behind her and kissed her nape, which lay invitingly bare under her short choppy hairstyle.

The imprint of his lips was like sizzling fire on her skin. She forced herself not to react, resolutely thinking of the lipstick stain on his shirt.

'Are you going to spend all evening here in the kitchen?' Cam asked plaintively. 'Philomena will be here in the morning to help you, Roxy. I thought we might spend an hour or so together, before you go to bed...I've some New Zealand travel brochures to show you.'

She was glad she wasn't facing him and couldn't see his expression as he mentioned the word 'bed'. Would the dark depths be glinting with rakish desire? Smiling with devilish mischief? Or would they be mocking her prudish hands-off-until-we're-married stance?

Was she making a mistake forcing him to wait? A man with his healthy sex drive might not *want* to wait. Might find it *impossible* to wait.

Maybe he'd already stopped waiting. She thought again of the lipstick stain on his collar, and groaned inwardly.

'You have a very sexy neck, you know,' Cam observed from behind.

She shivered. If she'd really meant something to him, she'd have been happy to turn round and melt into his arms.

Did she mean anything to him at all? A foolish hope fluttered.

Could she have been mistaken about the lipstick stain? Could it have been something else?

No... Her mouth twisted. She knew a lipstick stain when she saw it.

But—she bit down on her lip—surely any lipstick stain would have been removed in the wash? She hadn't noticed it, she realised, when she'd hung out the wet shirt in the first place.

Maybe her own lips had brushed against the collar as she'd reached up to pluck the dry shirt from the

line. She'd been wearing pink lipstick today herself—
in fact, she'd just applied fresh lipstick in readiness
for Cam's arrival home—and it had been windy this
afternoon, she recalled. The wind could have blown
the shirt, brushing it against her lips, leaving—

'And a very sexy behind,' Cam murmured.

She gave up. With a deep quivering breath she
swung round—to find Cam's gaze fastening on her
breasts, outlined by the white fitted top she was wearing.

Before he could pass a remark about her sexy
breasts, she said rather breathlessly, 'Okay, you win.
Show me the brochures.' If she could keep his mind
on their travel plans, it might dampen his lustful
urges—and her own weak-willed responses. She was
damned if she was going to give in to him, tempted
as she was. She still didn't trust him enough…and
that lipstick stain today, wherever it had come from,
had done nothing to help.

CHAPTER EIGHT

Two weeks before their wedding day, as they were sitting at the dining-room table enjoying one of Roxy's own culinary efforts—a surprisingly successful rack of lamb—Cam asked her, 'Do you think you could stand having a few people here next Sunday for a poolside barbecue lunch? I'd like my friends and work mates to meet my fiancée and our niece.'

Roxy's heart gave a double jump. 'Sure,' she said huskily, wondering why Cam would want his friends to meet her before they were married. So they wouldn't be surprised when he announced at work one day that he had a wife? She hid a sigh. A man in love would have had a more sentimental reason. He would simply have wanted to show off the love of his life.

Still, it was a thoughtful gesture…if a bit nerve-racking. His friends were bound to guess that this was no love match and that they were only marrying for the sake of their niece. When they heard that the wedding was to be a private ceremony, without any guests present, other than the two local witnesses, they'd be even more convinced .

Not that a private wedding meant that a couple couldn't be in love, Roxy reflected, recalling a friend who'd eloped to Hawaii with her boyfriend to avoid the fuss and expense of a wedding at home. And they'd both been madly in love.

Would Cam's friends wonder if *they* were madly in love?

Her lips curved in a wistful smile. Hardly likely, when it had all happened so quickly. Besides which, Cam had made it clear that love wasn't a necessary part of their marriage and he wouldn't be pretending that it was. And she, for her part, would be trying her best—for her own self-preservation—to hide the fact that she had stupidly fallen in love with *him*.

Would Cam want it to appear that cold-blooded? Or would he want to make out that it *was* a love match—and expect her to put on an act, too?

An act! She nearly laughed aloud. She wouldn't have to put on an act. But to show her feelings openly... How would that affect *her?*

The next day Cam had to drive up to Sydney for a business meeting, and because he had a dinner to attend in the evening, he stayed in town overnight.

Roxy hardly slept a wink that night, tired as she was after another busy day caring for the baby and preparing for the influx of visitors at the weekend. She tried her best not to think about what Cam might be doing in town, or the company he might be keeping, but the insidious thoughts kept coming, keeping her awake. Was his trip to the city purely business? Was his dinner in the evening a business dinner, or an intimate private dinner for two? Legitimate business dinner or not, had he brought one of his dinner companions—or another female altogether—back to his hotel room afterwards?

She groaned, blotting out the sickening images in her mind.

'Stop it, Roxy,' she growled in exasperation.

'You'll drive yourself mad.' Plumping up her pillows for the umpteenth time, she flung herself onto her back. But still she couldn't sleep. Her head was aching with the need for sleep, but it wouldn't come.

She blew out a tremulous sigh. It's pure hell, she thought ruefully, loving a man who doesn't love you. Loving a man you're not sure you can trust. Missing a man who's probably forgotten about you already, now that you're out of his sight. Out of sight, out of mind...

She squeezed her eyes shut.

It's only an overnight business trip, you poor fool. He'll be home in the morning, he said. You have to get some sleep! You don't want to look as if you've been lying awake all night worrying about him, imagining what he's been up to. Even if you have.

It seemed that the moment she did finally drift off to sleep, the baby woke her again, crying for her breakfast. Roxy dragged herself out of bed, feeling like death.

When Cam arrived home around ten, she'd just arrived back at the house herself, after taking Emma along the cliffs in her stroller for some fresh air. He found her in the kitchen, where she'd wheeled Emma to give her a drink of water and a biscuit.

As Emma munched contentedly on a dry cracker biscuit, Roxy turned to face the man she'd promised to marry.

Her heart lurched at the sight of him. He looked so damned sexy! He was wearing a white business shirt without a tie, and the top two buttons were undone, showing a mouth-drying glimpse of tanned flesh. Under his heavy brows and dark wavy hair, his glittering black eyes burned into hers, showing no sign at all of a late, dissipated night or lack of sleep—as hers must, she was glumly aware, after no dissipation whatsoever!

'Good trip?' she asked carelessly, and gasped as he grabbed her by the arms, swept her up against him and kissed her on the lips. A brief but very real kiss.

'Missed you,' he murmured as he drew back and let her go. But he said it lightly, she noted with a quiver. Perhaps he felt that he had to say it. 'Mmm...it went okay, I guess. The meeting was a bit drawn out, and Mirella had forgotten to put some vital papers into my briefcase for me. Normally she's pretty efficient.'

Roxy felt her nerve-ends tense at the mention of Mirella, and at his defense of her. 'Your secretary didn't go with you?' she asked innocently, eyeing him from under her lashes, keeping her eyes carefully shadowed.

There was a pause before Cam answered. 'Would you be jealous if she had?' he asked with a lift of an eyebrow.

'Jealous?' She gave a quick laugh. 'Of course not,' she lied. 'Why...should I be?'

As she probed the glinting black eyes, they became hooded and remote under her scrutiny.

'I told you that I was committed to this marriage, Roxy...and to *you*.' He shook his head. 'You still don't trust me, do you?'

She shrugged. 'Your brother warned me not to. And with good reason,' she added with a jut of her chin, remembering with a pang the way Cam had dumped her for that stunning brunette at her sister's wedding; remembering the raven-haired Belinda he'd flaunted a year later at Emma's christening.

'Circumstances were different then,' Cam said with a dismissive jerk of his shoulder. 'You had your life and I had mine. Now our lives are about to converge…' He glanced down at the baby. She thought he was about to add, *for our niece's sake,* but he didn't. 'Hi, princess,' he said instead. 'Got a kiss for your Uncle Cam?'

He bent to kiss the child's cheek, not bothering about the messy face Emma presented to him. Roxy, melting despite herself, felt a wave of warmth at his genuine show of affection for Emma. He did love his niece. As much as she did. And Emma, after all, was the one most in need of love, having had it snatched away from her so tragically, at such an early, vital age.

'The day we get married,' Cam said, straightening, 'I want us to be Mummy and Daddy to her, Roxy…not Aunt and Uncle. We're going to be real parents…a real family…from that day on.'

But there was still over a week and a half to go, he was reminding her. She still had time to back out.

'I can't wait to be Mummy to Emma,' she said without hesitation. She wanted to add, *And I can't wait to be your wife,* but she couldn't bring herself to say it. She still wasn't sure enough of him. He still had time to back out, too.

Her answer, however, appeared to have pleased him. He smiled, his eyes crinkling in a way that tugged at her heart. 'I'll be home all day today,' he announced. 'I want to clean out the swimming pool and do some clearing in the garden.' A self-mocking curve quirked his lip. 'I want to show my friends that I'm not only capable of caring for a baby, but a home as well.'

The perfect father and family man, in other words. Roxy noticed that he hadn't specifically mentioned *her.*

When Friday's mail was delivered there was an airmail letter for her. She'd had all her mail forwarded to Raeburns' Nest since she'd been staying with Cam.

The envelope was from Harvard University. Her eyes widened. She only knew one person at Harvard…Professor Arnold Bergman, the eminent archeologist. She'd worked with him a couple of times, at digs in Mexico and Peru. But her university had arranged those field trips. He'd never personally written to her before.

Why would he be writing to her now? A lowly Australian archeologist? *Ex*-archeologist.

She slit open the envelope and pulled out the handwritten letter inside. It was an invitation to join the professor's team at a dig in northern Peru, where an exquisitely crafted gold goblet had been unearthed in an area previously unexplored and unexcavated. The find opened up all kinds of exciting possibilities, the professor pointed out.

The dig of a lifetime!

She expected to feel a burst of excitement, a wave of temptation, but she didn't. Not even a quiver. If the invitation had come a year ago she would have jumped at it. But she had other priorities now—other even more exciting discoveries waiting to be made.

She glanced at baby Emma playing on the floor with her toys. Yes…other things excited her more now…the baby's irresistible smile…the way her niece held out her arms to be picked up…the anticipation of hearing Emma's first words…seeing her first steps…even spying a new tooth.

And there was Cam… He excited her, too, as no man ever had. She wanted to be his wife with all her heart, despite her lingering doubts about his commitment to her.

She slipped the letter back into its envelope, not needing to think twice about turning down the professor's flattering offer. And she'd be doing it without a flicker of regret.

She found some notepaper and wrote back immediately, thanking the professor for his kind invitation and explaining that she'd given up field work permanently because she was about to get married and wanted to devote all her time from now on to her new husband and the orphaned niece they planned to adopt. He'd be surprised, no doubt—she'd been so dedicated to her field work for so long, particularly over the past year—but hopefully he'd understand her reasons and accept them without rancour.

She was strongly tempted to show Cam the professor's letter and her reply—with her reasons for declining the offer. That should convince him as nothing else could that she was serious about giving up her field work to stay at home with Emma and her new husband.

But she stopped herself in time, worried that Cam might think she was only telling him so that he'd feel obliged to let her go.

Best not to tell him at all.

Next morning, Saturday—the day before their pool-

side barbecue—she left the baby with Cam and drove
into Kiama to secretly post the letter while she was
buying the steaks, salad vegetables and other provi-
sions for the party, including ingredients for a cheese-
cake she intended to make that afternoon. Cam had
already bought the drinks and Philomena had offered
to make some dips and savories. Mary was coming
to help them take care of the baby.

As her letter to Professor Bergman dropped into
the mailbox she felt a sense of release. She'd burned
her bridges and didn't regret it for a second.

Sunday dawned bright, clear and pleasantly hot—perfect for a poolside barbecue. The first one to arrive—
half an hour early, catching Roxy before she'd had a
chance to change out of her grubby work shorts and
food-spattered shirt into something more present-
able—was Cam's secretary, Mirella.

'Oh, am I early?' the glamorous brunette purred as
Cam brought her into the kitchen, where Roxy was
putting the finishing touches to a pasta salad. Mirella's dark gaze raked over Roxy from head to toe,
making no attempt to hide the derisive gleam in her
eye, or her gloating half smile.

Roxy didn't apologize for her messy appearance,
refusing to give Cam's secretary—*or was she more
than his secretary?*—the satisfaction. She returned the
girl's condescending look with cool, unblinking blue
eyes, showing no reaction to the eye-boggling sight
Mirella was presenting herself.

The shapely brunette had obviously come prepared
to knock out the eyes of all her male colleagues and
to make their wives and girlfriends squirm with

envy—or embarrassment. She was wearing a revealing coral-red cut-off top that exposed her ample cleavage and tanned midriff, and a multicoloured wraparound skirt which Roxy suspected would mysteriously unravel the moment Mirella and the other guests were gathered at the poolside. No doubt she was wearing a wispy bikini underneath.

'Cam, why don't you take Mirella out to the pool?' she heard herself suggesting sweetly. 'Mary's out there with Emma. I'll just finish this salad.'

'Let me finish it, love,' Philomena offered from the other side of the bench, but sorely as Roxy was tempted to flee the kitchen, she refused the kindly offer, doggedly staying until the salad was complete. Only then did she dash to her room to wash her face and hands—she'd showered earlier—and to change into casual party gear. She chose white ankle-length pants and a sleeveless scoop-necked top in a cornflower blue to match her eyes.

She didn't bother with make-up, other than some fresh pink lipstick, and there was nothing much she could do about her hair but run a brush through it and hope for the best.

She wouldn't need a swimsuit. She didn't intend to go swimming. As Cam's future bride, she wanted to spend the day meeting and mingling with his friends and work mates…and as hostess, it was up to her to keep their guests supplied with food and drink. Later, after they'd gone, maybe she'd take a dip then.

By the time she joined Cam and Mirella by the pool, others were beginning to arrive. They were a friendly crowd, Roxy quickly found, and they seemed as anxious to meet and get to know her as they were to see and fuss over the baby.

Roxy was pleasantly surprised to find that she liked everyone she met. Nobody embarrassed her with awkward questions. Nobody voiced aloud any snide speculation as to why she and Cam might have chosen to marry, or why they were planning a small private wedding ceremony, without any guests. They just seemed to accept it. To accept *her*. They would have heard, of course, about Hamish and Serena, Cam's brother and her sister, and they seemed to accept that a big wedding wouldn't be appropriate.

Everyone but Mirella made her feel at ease.

The flamboyant brunette had already disrobed, and was reclining in a lounger at the poolside, showing off a scandalously scanty rope bikini and a lot of smooth golden flesh. She was making no attempt to mingle, obviously expecting others to gravitate to her—which they did, Roxy noticed. Not just the young single males, either. Some of the married guys were hovering around the pool, too, surreptitiously ogling her.

Cam appeared to be keeping an eye on his glamorous secretary as well. A jealous eye? Roxy wondered with a quiver. An admiring eye? A *possessive* eye? Yet he was being a good host at the same time, constantly moving around, ensuring that everyone had a drink and that nobody was feeling left out.

He was keeping his eye on her, too, Roxy realised poignantly, being suitably attentive, as a loving fiancé should be, and making sure she was never alone or left out. It warmed her a little, even as she brooded about his relationship with his dark-eyed secretary.

At lunchtime Cam cooked the barbecue with the

help of his general manager, Peter. Peter's wife, Ann, helped Roxy and Philomena bring out the salads and other food. Tables were already set up outside, some shaded by sun umbrellas, others in the dappled shade of the trees. It was a perfect mid-December day, hot without being unpleasantly humid, with a gentle breeze, and not a cloud in the sky.

Roxy found herself enjoying the day more and more as the afternoon wore on—enjoying the company, the laughter, the good spirits. Only Mirella's presence spoiled it.

There were quite a few people in the pool by now, but the eye-catching Mirella remained in her banana lounge, sipping champagne and deepening her tan.

It wasn't until late in the afternoon, after a few of the guests had left, that Mirella finally rose—a trifle unsteadily—and lowered herself into the pool.

So she does occasionally get her hair wet, Roxy thought with grudging admiration, sighing as the golden-limbed, raven-haired siren struck out across the pool. Having no wish to stay around watching her, Roxy moved away to mingle with the remaining guests.

When she returned some time later, she saw Cam standing at the edge of the pool, openly watching Mirella in the water. The girl was floating on her back, gently kicking her long legs, her black hair swirling round her, a tanned arm raised in a languid wave. Cam lifted his hand in an answering salute.

Roxy felt a piercing stab of hurt. On the very day Cam was introducing his future bride to his friends, he had eyes only for his sexy secretary!

As she approached the pool, one of Cam's male

colleagues—it was Peter, his general manager—
joined Cam at the poolside. With a glance at Mirella,
Peter leaned close to Cam and said something that
made his boss smile—indulgently, it seemed to Roxy.
Cam was still watching Mirella.

Composing herself, she forced herself to join them,
forced herself to comment lightly, 'It's a wonder
some guy hasn't snapped up your secretary by now,
Cam. She's quite a dish, isn't she?'

'Yeah…' It was Peter who spoke, turning to her
with a rueful grin. 'And I'd better stop watching before my wife catches me. Time we were going home
anyway. Thanks for a terrific day, both of you. Great
to meet you, Roxy.' He gave Cam a friendly punch
on the arm and melted away in search of his wife.

Cam glanced down at Roxy. 'Mirella's had a bit
too much to drink.' He spoke in a wry drawl. 'I
thought it wise to keep a wary eye on her. We don't
want a drowning on our—oh, Roxy, I'm sorry.' He
looked genuinely dismayed at his inadvertent reminder of the family boating tragedy. 'That was un-
forgivably thoughtless of me.' He reached out a hand
to her but she dodged it.

'Don't worry about it,' she said stiffly, and swung
away. Let him think it was the reminder of Serena
and Hamish that was ruffling her, not her doubts
about *him*.

She drew in a tremulous breath. Could she believe
him? That he was only watching Mirella to avoid a
mishap in the pool? He'd been eyeing his flamboyant
secretary before she even entered the water!

By now the sun was low in the sky and the few
remaining guests were preparing to leave, keen to set

off before dark. Some had come all the way from
Sydney, others from Wollongong and the towns
around. There was the usual last-minute flurry as cou-
ples scurried around searching for belongings and
handbags and making their final farewells.

When everyone had finally gone Roxy realised that
she hadn't said goodbye to Mirella. When had the girl
left the pool and slipped away? Had she said goodbye
to Cam? Roxy couldn't bring herself to ask him. But
she did make a brief check of the pool, to make sure
his sexy secretary wasn't lying on the bottom!

Capable Mary had already fed little Emma and put
her down in her cot, and now she was ready to leave
for home herself. After thanking her and seeing her
off, Roxy and Cam spent the next hour or so helping
Philomena clean up the mess, nibbling leftovers as
they worked, which was all they felt like for dinner.

After Philomena had gone home, too, Cam turned
to Roxy with a smile and suggested they both relax
over a cup of coffee in the family room.

'I think we've both earned the chance to put our
feet up. I'll make it,' he offered.

Roxy thought of declining his offer and going
straight to bed, but heard herself answering, 'I'll just
go to my room and fetch a sweater.' The night air
had a faint chill. Unless it was the thought of being
alone with Cam that was making her shiver.

Cam caught her arm as she turned to go, swinging
her round to face him. 'You were wonderful, Roxy.'
There was a tender warmth in his eyes that she hadn't
seen before. Not directed at her, at any rate. 'They all
adored you.'

She swallowed. He wasn't saying that *he* adored

her. 'They're very nice people,' she said with genuine feeling. 'They seem very fond of you, too,' she added. Especially his stunning secretary.

'I've a great team, on the whole. You'll have to come to the plant with me one day, so I can show you around.' He caught her face in his hands and looked into her eyes for a heart-stopping moment, his black gaze showed a different kind of warmth now, a glittering warmth that set her pulses racing. And then he kissed her, long and hungrily, on the lips.

'Thank you for all the hard work you put into to-day,' he murmured as he lifted his head. 'You must be worn-out.'

She shook her head, her eyes faintly dazed. *Only breathless from your kiss,* she thought shakily, feeling the same weakness in his arms that she always felt.

'Now…' Cam sighed as he reluctantly released her. 'Let me put on our coffee before I forget that I'm supposed to wait until our wedding night.'

'I'll get my sweater,' she breathed, her body trembling as she headed for her room. So he still wanted her. He still desired her. He didn't adore her…he didn't love her…but he did want her in his bed.

As she passed the master bedroom she noticed that the door was wide-open. A light from inside the room caught her eye—Cam's bedside lamp, casting its golden glow across the big bed.

There was a reclining figure on the bed. A woman's tanned, curvaceous figure—with absolutely nothing on!

CHAPTER NINE

ROXY came to a shocked halt. Mirella! There was no mistaking the raven hair spilling over the pillows, the sexy curves, the long golden legs. She'd been exposed to Mirella's flamboyant charms all day!

But not *this* exposed.

Mirella's stringy bikini lay discarded on the carpet beside the bed.

Roxy felt a scorching heat in her cheeks—and a burning ache deep inside. Had Cam brought his secretary in here to his bedroom himself? To let her sleep off the champagne she'd overindulged in?

Had Mirella, before she'd fallen asleep, undressed and left the door open…deliberately? Hoping Cam's fiancée would see her in his bed?

A wave of bitter anger welled up inside her.

Cam wouldn't dare! He wouldn't be so blatant, only days before their wedding! He'd never take such a risk, with so much at stake. With his niece at stake!

But if *he* hadn't brought his secretary in here, or invited her in, how did Mirella know where his bedroom was? *Because she'd been here before?*

Roxy shivered—and it had nothing to do with the coolness in the air. But it *was* quite chilly now, she realised in the next breath—too chilly for sleeping in the nude. She took a deep, rallying breath. Much as she hated the idea, she marched into Cam's bedroom and pulled a sheet over his naked secretary, and the duvet over that. Not only for warmth, but for decency! Mirella didn't stir.

Then she stomped back to the kitchen to confront Cam.

'I thought you were going to put a sweater on,' he said, glancing up as he poured coffee into two mugs.

Roxy, flushing with mingled hurt and fury, gulped in a deep calming breath. 'I thought it was more important to put a sweater on your secretary. Or at least a cover.'

Cam went still. He stared at her. 'What the hell are you talking about?'

'Mirella's fast asleep in your bed...and she's stark naked. You didn't know?' she asked sweetly, hiding the blackness in her heart.

'No, of course I didn't know. But I'm not surprised,' he said coolly.

Roxy blinked, a deep pang knifing through her. 'You're not surprised she's in your bed?'

He shrugged. 'Nothing Mirella does surprises me. She loves to be the life of the party and she tends to drink too much.' He turned back to the coffee. 'Best to let her sleep it off. She's in no fit state to drive home anyway. I'll run her home when she wakes up—in her car—then get a cab back.'

'And if she doesn't wake up?'

'Then I'll find somewhere else to sleep tonight.'

Roxy's eyes searched his face. Would he?

Suddenly she'd had enough. More than enough! 'Look...I'm asleep on my feet myself.' She winced at the strangled sounds coming from her throat. 'I think I'll give the coffee a miss...it might keep me awake.'

She didn't want to be kept awake, listening throughout the night for sounds from across the passage. She wanted to be in a dead sleep and know nothing about it.

Cam looked at her as if he were about to say something, but ended up nodding and waving her off. 'I'll sit up for a while…in case I have to drive Mirella home later. But don't be surprised if she's here for breakfast.' He grimaced.

Roxy gave a weak laugh. 'Oh, nothing your secretary does would shock me,' she quipped, and scuttled off to her room, not even glancing into the master bedroom before diving into her safe little den and closing the door firmly behind her.

She didn't fall asleep straight away. She lay in bed, forcing herself to stay awake, listening against her will for sounds of Mirella stirring to life…or Cam tiptoeing into his bedroom. But sheer exhaustion caught up with her in the end, before she could find out if Mirella had woken in time for Cam to drive her home…or if she'd stayed all night.

When she woke the next morning—for a change it wasn't the baby who woke her—she heard voices in the passage. A man's deep voice and a woman's voice, richly sensual and laced with sultry laughter.

So Mirella *had* stayed all night. *Where had Cam slept?*

Hot prickles seared her cheeks. Wherever he *said* he'd slept, would she be able to believe him? Whatever story he spun, would she be a fool to believe that nothing had happened?

She heard their voices and footsteps growing

fainter, then the bang of the side door, followed by silence. They'd left the house. Together.

A moment later she heard a car drive off.

She dragged herself out of bed. She needed coffee *now,* and badly! She didn't even bother to brush her hair or pull a gown over her Snoopy nightshirt— who'd see her? She'd be back in her room with her coffee—or dressed, attending to the baby—before Cam came back from Mirella's. Unless he'd gone straight on to work.

It was only 7:00 a.m., but sometimes he did go off to the plant this early. Having had Friday off, he might want to catch up on lost time.

Mirella was with him.

She growled, like an animal in pain. Would she ever be able to trust him? She loved him...she loved him despite her doubts about him...but how would she ever be able to give in fully to the passion she felt for him when she was so unsure of him? How would she ever be able to show him, let alone tell him in words, how much she loved him? Holding back on her emotions was the only protection she had.

As she lifted the kettle to pour boiling water into the coffeepot, the kitchen door burst open and Cam breezed in. She nearly dropped the kettle. As it was, boiling water splashed onto the bench, and over her hand.

'Ouch!' She put down the kettle down with a clatter. 'Did you have to burst in like that?' Knowing how she must look was hurting her more than the stinging burn on her hand.

'Sorry...I didn't know you were in here.' Cam was at her side in one long stride, seizing her hand.

'Here…put it under the cold water tap—it might help.' He was turning on the tap with his free hand.

'Look, it's fine, don't fuss.' The touch of his hand was both agony and bliss. All she wanted to do was escape. 'Just pour me a coffee and I'll go back to bed until Emma wakes up. I'm still half asleep.'

But he already had her hand under the tap, holding it there as the cold water gushed over it. 'You look gorgeous to me.' He grinned down at her. 'All pink and dewy-eyed and rumpled. Have a good sleep?'

'Like a baby,' she said lightly. 'And you?' She slid a look up at him, but instead of seeing signs of guilt or embarrassment, she saw humour instead, his dark eyes twinkling as his lips curved in a crooked smile.

'As well as a six-foot-plus male can sleep in an armchair.'

An armchair? She felt a whoosh of relief, even as she wondered if she could believe him. 'Mirella slept the night through, did she?' she asked carelessly, snatching her hand back and shaking it dry.

'Must have. Bounced up bright and bushy-tailed this morning, ready to go to work…after calling in home to change into something more business-like than that wraparound skirt and skimpy top—which at least covered her better than those pieces of string she called a bikini. I've just seen her off home. She's borrowed one of my sweaters.' His lip quirked. 'I don't know how she does it.'

Roxy was tempted to ask, *Does what? Fill your sweater?* But she had a feeling he was referring to the way Mirella had bounced up bright-eyed and ready for work, after all the champagne she'd downed the day before.

'Thanks,' she mumbled as he poured her a coffee and handed it to her. As she turned to go, Cam followed her into the passage.

'I'll strip my bed and put the sheets in the washing machine before I change for work,' he offered. 'It's the least I can do to help.'

'Don't worry, I'll see to it,' she said, though the thought of touching the sheets his secretary had been sleeping between made her shudder.

'No, it's my problem, not yours,' Cam insisted. 'They're a mess. I've never seen so much make-up and mascara, or whatever—I'll have to scrub the sheets and pillow slips before I put them into the tub.'

Roxy pursed her lips, her face heating. Was it only make-up he wanted to scrub clean? She plunged into her bedroom, blotting out such tormenting thoughts. She had to start believing him, trusting him, or she'd never survive this marriage!

CHAPTER TEN

THE rest of the day flew by. With the baby to look after she barely had a moment to spare…and mercifully little time to think. Edgy as she was, Roxy was finding every second she spent with little Emma a pure joy. With each day that passed she was bonding more closely with the beloved niece who would soon be legally her daughter.

She made a special effort for dinner, preparing roast lamb with all the trimmings and baking Cam's favourite dessert, a creamy rice pudding. Cam opened a bottle of vintage claret, 'to do it justice'.

It was a perfect evening…at least on the surface. They discussed the day's events, laughed over the baby's latest tricks, argued over politics and put finishing touches to their New Zealand itinerary. Then Cam suggested watching a late documentary on television. It was on the Aztecs of Mexico…Roxy's specialty.

She eyed him in mingled surprise and suspicion. Was he testing her willpower? Or just being thoughtful, knowing she'd be interested in the program? She made herself believe the latter, especially when no mocking glances or taunting comments came her way. Cam seemed genuinely interested in the program himself. She settled down to enjoy it.

Sexual tension simmered below the companionable surface, heightening her awareness of him. Each day, she mused wistfully, she could feel herself being drawn closer to him…falling a little more in love with him…yearning for him as she'd never yearned for any man before.

It *would* work, if she didn't expect too much. It *would!*

Then why was she trembling? Why did she feel so on edge?

She sighed, hardly noticing the program unfolding before her, her mind too intent on the man beside her. Blissfully happy as she was with the new life she'd chosen, her doubts about Cam—based solely, she had to admit, on past experience and some unproven suspicions since—were stretching her taut nerves to breaking point.

By the next evening, with only four days to go to their wedding day, she was nearly bursting with tension and uncertainty. Could she go through with it?

She thought of the child they both loved. The child who deserved two parents again…two parents who loved her equally.

She had to!

'Ouch!' She pricked her finger as she sewed a new button onto one of her shirts. She was all fingers and thumbs tonight.

She glanced up and caught Cam watching her from the armchair opposite, as he flicked through a business journal.

'You're a bundle of nerves, Roxy.' He frowned. 'Getting cold feet, now that the big day's nearly on us? There's still time to back out.'

'Is that what *you* want? For me to give up any claim to Emma and go back to my field work and out of your life?' Her voice was higher than usual, and she could feel that the colour in her cheeks was equally high.

'No, it's damned well not what I want. But if it's what you want, Roxy, I want you to say so now—I don't want another wife who walks out on me the minute she has my ring on her finger.'

Roxy gulped. Did he still not trust her to keep to her word? Was he still afraid that she might want to go back to her globetrotting career after they were married? Had he been testing her last night after all, with that Aztec program?

Or was there more to it?

'If you're worried that I'll demand money from you, Cam, if we get divorced, you can forget it,' she said stiffly. 'I'm not after your money. I'll sign anything you want to prove it. I just want my niece!' *And you, damn it, and you!*

Something flickered in the black depths, then died. 'Once we're married,' Cam said with cold precision, 'there'll be no question of divorce. You're either in for the long haul, Roxy, or you're out. You have four days to decide!'

'I'm in,' she whispered. 'If you're genuinely committed to this marriage, Cam, then so am I.' Her eyes gleamed as she challenged him with the word 'committed'.

He leaned forward in his chair. 'Are you committed to *me,* Roxy? Or is our niece the only reason you're marrying me?' His tone was faintly mocking, his dark eyes, lit by glinting pinpricks of light, difficult to read.

As her lips parted, he said in a soft drawl, 'You've given me the impression, once or twice, Roxy, that you do feel…something. That you might even want *me* as part of the package.' His gaze was on her mouth now, and she resisted an almost overwhelming urge to moisten her lips with a flick of her tongue. 'I might be wrong, but…' A smile edged upwards. 'Sometimes I get the impression that you want me, Roxy, as much as I want you.'

She felt herself trembling. *Want*…always want, she thought with a poignant glance up at him…never *love.*

'Maybe I want more than just—just—' She floundered. Snatching in a quick breath, she burst out, 'I want a husband who's not just committed to his marriage and his children, but to *me!* To his *wife!'*

As the cry wrenched from her, Cam left his chair and jerked her to her feet. His fingers were like steel bands round her arms. 'I *am* totally committed to you, Roxy.' His face tightened, as if he found it a difficult thing to admit. 'You're the best thing that's ever happened to me. And if you'll only commit yourself totally to *me,*' he growled savagely, 'I'll show you I mean it.'

The best thing…show you I mean it… She felt her bones melting.

'You're saying…I'll be the only woman in your life?' she pressed huskily. He still hadn't used the word 'love'—and she wasn't going to force it from him. Words were easy enough when forced from you. But not so easy, apparently, when you had to think them up yourself. When you had to speak from the heart.

'That's precisely what I mean.'

But he still wasn't telling her precisely how he *felt.*

He still wasn't telling her he *cared* for her, *felt* something for her. As she watched, she saw a fiery spark kindle in the black depths, and a playful quirk lift his lips. 'Like me to show you, Roxy? Prove it to you? Or are you still going to make me wait?'

'Cam, I...' Her hands fluttered as she hesitated. If he really cared for her he *would* wait. Unless he was the type of man—a twinge pierced her—who *couldn't* wait. The type who needed a sexual outlet; the type who could love a wife, or believe he loved her, yet still have affairs on the side.

She gazed up at him, her eyes huge blue pools in her fineboned face. It had suddenly become vitally important to know precisely how he did feel about her.

'It—it would mean a lot to me, Cam, if you *could* wait until our wedding night,' she whispered. If she'd been more sure of him, she realised pensively, she wouldn't *want* him to wait. *She* wouldn't want to wait, either.

She lowered her eyes, shifting restlessly in his arms. If she could find a way to make him believe that she was totally committed to this marriage...to show him she had no intention of ever abandoning him or little Emma to go chasing off to another remote dig somewhere—maybe he would begin to trust her *then*. Maybe, once his mind was set at rest, he might even admit that he had some real feeling for her.

If he *had* any real feeling for her.

'I'd better finish sewing on this button and then go to bed,' she said, wriggling out of his arms and settling down again in her armchair.

Cam was never going to fully trust her—or allow himself to fall in love with her—until he was convinced that she wasn't going to get itchy feet and want her old life back.

Maybe she should have shown him Professor Bergman's invitation and her letter of refusal after all. But it was too late now. She'd already posted her letter and she'd destroyed the professor's invitation. If she told him about it now, would he believe her?

She would just have to find some other way to convince him that she was serious about settling down for good.

Her mind raced. Already an idea was beginning to form. Of course! It was something she'd always wanted to do when she finally retired from her field work and settled down. Something she'd never had a chance to do, living in a small city flat, and being seldom been at home anyway. If she could give Cam some concrete evidence of what she planned to do— keeping it as a surprise, perhaps, until their wedding day—surely that would convince him?

She felt excitement building as she thought of an even more convincing way to set Cam's mind at rest. While she was in Sydney she would put her flat up for sale! She'd been holding onto it as a safety net in case her marriage to Cam never took place. But the time had come to take a leap of faith—to show Cam just how serious she was about settling down permanently at Raeburns' Nest.

She glanced up at him through her lashes. He was already sinking down opposite her, scooping up his business magazine. But he wasn't looking at it. He was looking at *her*.

She felt a tremor shake through her. She would have given much to know what he was thinking. She waited for a breathless second but he didn't speak.

Taking a couple of deep breaths, she asked, 'Cam…would you mind if I popped up to Sydney tomorrow?'

He looked surprised at her change of tack. 'No, of course I don't mind. You must have shopping to do…clothes to buy…friends to see.'

'Yes…' She hid a secret smile. She *would* be doing some shopping. But not for clothes. She didn't need any new clothes. She had formal dresses and leisure gear in her Sydney flat that she'd rarely worn. She'd been too busy travelling and lecturing and fossicking around in the dirt.

She hugged her secret. Cam needn't know that she'd be heading for a good bookshop, not the fashion boutiques. The books she was planning to buy would, she hoped, be a delightful surprise for him on their wedding day.

Should she keep the sale of her flat as a surprise for him, too? Maybe not, she decided after a moment's hesitation. Best to give Cam some proof now that she was serious about severing her links with Sydney—with her past life.

'Cam, there's something else I want to do while I'm in Sydney.' She faced him determinedly. 'Put my flat up for sale. I won't be needing it any more…not now that I'll be getting married and living permanently at Raeburns' Nest.' If that didn't convince him she was serious about staying with him, what would?

'Well…if you're sure you want to sell it.' Cam seemed pleased, she thought. 'You'll always have my

apartment—*our* apartment,' he corrected, 'if you want
to go up to town. It's right in the heart of the city.'
He paused. 'But why not wait until after our honeymoon? You'll have more time then. You'll need a
couple of days, won't you, to find a good agent and
prepare your flat for sale?'

Roxy considered. She certainly didn't want to be
away from Emma for a couple of days and nights at
this crucial stage of their life together.

She opened her mouth, ready to agree with Cam
and put off the sale until later. But something stopped
her.

She bit down on her lip. The flat was already neat
and tidy. And she already knew a good agent—the
man who'd sold the flat to her father a few years ago.
He'd be familiar with the flat and she could leave the
keys with him…trust everything to him.

Her heartbeat was quickening. A new idea was
forming in her mind. A crazy idea…an outrageous
idea, but it would be a perfect way to find out, once
and for all, if she could trust Cam with another
woman!

And it would mean she wouldn't have to be away
from little Emma—or from Cam, either—for more
than a few short hours. But Cam would think that she
was still in Sydney, staying at her flat for two nights!

If she managed to pull it off.

Could she fool Cam? That was the question. She
hid an impish smile. She'd fooled her Uni friends
once. It would be fun to see if she *could* pull it off.
It would only be for a couple of days and it would
hurt no one—least of all little Emma. The baby would

recognise her, even if Cam didn't. She would make sure her niece did!

'Like me to drive up with you and give you a hand?' Cam offered. 'I'll ask Mary to come and mind Emma for a couple of days.'

Her eyes flared in panic. '*Both* of us leave Emma? Oh, I wouldn't want to do that! Not so soon after…' she gulped and hastened on. 'One of us should stay with our niece. She's only just beginning to feel safe and comfortable with us.' She was worried enough about leaving the baby herself, even for a few short hours.

Besides, her new plan would go up in smoke if Cam came with her.

'I can manage—truly,' she assured him. 'Mary can look after Emma while you're at work, but you should be here, too…for part of the day and overnight.'

'Yes…I guess you're right.'

Something in his tone made her bend her head swiftly, reaching down for her sewing basket to avoid his eye. Was he still unsure of her? Had he sensed that she had something else in mind?

But he couldn't! How could he? She shook off the unnerving thought. She had more reason to be unsure of *him!*

Her heart gave a quiver. Would he miss her? Or was he already feeling excited at the prospect of being alone for a couple of nights? Mirella's voluptuous image rose to taunt her.

She kept her eyes hidden from him as she gathered up her shirt and sewing basket. 'I'd better go to bed so I can make an early start,' she said, jumping up. She wanted time to think…to plan.

She fled from the room before she could change her mind.

She set off for Sydney the next morning while Cam was giving Emma her breakfast. Mary was due to arrive shortly, allowing Cam to go off to work. He was planning to come home around lunchtime, he'd told Roxy, to make sure that Emma wasn't missing them both too much.

He'd asked her to call him now and then and let him know how things were going. She could reach him on his mobile phone if he wasn't at home. She'd already asked him not to call *her,* telling him that she'd be in and out of the flat a lot and would probably stay overnight with friends. She didn't have a mobile phone, luckily, so he couldn't reach her that way. That would have been disastrous, since she was going to be in same house with him!

She ran her tongue over her lips as she steered her baby Mazda out onto the road. Her lips still felt bruised from the passionate kiss Cam had given her before she left. The intensity of his kiss had prompted her to ask—naively perhaps—for reassurances.

'Only four days to our wedding day, Cam…' She'd injected a teasing note into her voice to cover her doubts. 'You honestly think you'll be able to stick to just one woman from now on? That *is* what being committed to marriage means…isn't it?'

His answer came promptly, without hesitation. 'There's been no one else but you, Roxy, since the first day I set eyes on you.'

No one else? She nearly recoiled in his arms. What about the brunette at Serena's wedding? What about the brunettes she'd seen him with since? Belinda? Mirella?

An ironic smile surfaced briefly. 'I'm not saying there haven't been other women. I'm saying there hasn't been another woman who has meant anything to me.' The words ground from him, a glinting intensity in his eye. 'You touched something in me, Roxy, the first time we met, but—' he blew out a sigh '—I guess I was still raw from my marriage to Kimberley. I decided to back off before it was too late. It was best, I believed then, not to get…involved.'

Her eyes wavered under his. Was that why he'd dumped her at Serena's wedding and gone off with another woman? So that she wouldn't have a chance to get emotionally involved herself, and start expecting anything of him? She sighed, hiding the pain in her eyes. Well, she hadn't waited. She hadn't expected anything of him. But her emotions, sadly, hadn't been so easy to brush off.

As she swung her zippy Mazda onto the main highway to Sydney, she recalled how the baby had squawked for attention at that point, and Cam— relieved no doubt—had turned away before she could ask any questions about the wife who'd run out on him.

A shadow touched her face. Cam so rarely mentioned his ex-wife, so rarely opened up about her or about what had gone wrong between them. Roxy had no idea if he still had feelings for Kimberley—if he wished, deep down, that he had his runaway wife back, rather than being lumbered with his baby niece's unglamorous aunt.

There's been no one else but you, Roxy, he'd said.

But had he simply told her what he thought a nervous bride-to-be needed to hear?

Her eyes gleamed as she hunched over the wheel. Maybe, in the next day or two, she would find out.

She drove straight to the agent's office in outer Sydney to sign him up and leave him with a key. Then she headed for a particular bookshop, where she quickly found exactly what she was looking for. By late morning she was back at her flat packing a bag— a weekend bag that Cam had never seen—and beginning work on her transformation.

An hour later she was ready. She sat at her dressing-table, staring at the stranger in the mirror...a dark-eyed siren in a slinky red dress. It was a dress she'd bought two years ago for one express purpose and she hadn't worn it since. She preferred less flamboyant gear. But on the woman in the mirror it looked just right. Perfect.

The face staring back at her was vaguely familiar...yet vastly different from the one she was used to seeing. The teased black wig and dark brown contact lenses had transformed her, while the carefully applied face powder, blusher, glossy red lipstick and dramatic eye make-up—thick eyebrow pencil, smouldering black eyeliner, lash-lengthening mascara and smoky eye shadow—were the pièce de résistance, converting her from a freshfaced, blue-eyed blonde into a provocative, raven-haired vamp.

'Hi, Vivien,' she said aloud, lowering her normal voice a notch to give it a new sultry element. 'Ready for the ride?'

She'd appeared as the dark-eyed Vivien only once

before…at an end of year party at Uni. She'd pretended to be her nonexistent first cousin Vivien, and had turned up alone, making out that Roxy was running late for the party. Nobody had seen through her dramatic disguise. Nobody had recognised her. She'd had marvellous fun until her friends, realising finally that Roxy hadn't turned up, had begun to get suspicious. She'd dropped her false voice then, laughed at them, and they'd woken up to who she was, squealing in disbelief.

But if Cam wasn't *expecting* Roxy…if he was expecting Roxy's look-alike first cousin—

Roxy gave a mischievous grin and picked up the phone.

'Cam Raeburn.'

'Cam, it's Roxy…'

'Roxy! How are you going?'

He sounded so pleased to hear from her that she felt a momentary qualm, flushing as she caught sight of the vampish Vivien in the mirror.

'I've done some shopping already,' she told him in a rush, 'and now I'm cleaning up the flat. There's an agent arriving shortly to look it over.' *Only I won't be here when he comes.* 'He—he thinks he might even have a possible buyer already—a young couple who can't come to see it until tomorrow.'

Her voice trembled at the white lie. She'd asked the agent not to put it on the market until after the weekend. Hopefully he'd come up with a genuine buyer quickly. He'd been highly optimistic.

'So you'll have to stay the extra day.'

Was that disappointment in Cam's voice? Was he

missing her already? she wondered hopefully. Or was he worried about little Emma missing her?

Emma won't *have* to miss me, she thought with a shivery thrill of anticipation. And I won't have to pine for her, either…or for Cam, for that matter. I'll be right there with them…only they won't know it.

If she managed to pull it off.

She smiled into the mirror, and Vivien smiled back, a wicked, scarlet smile.

'I'll only be away for two nights,' she said lightly. 'Cam, there's something else,' she gulped out before she could change her mind and scrub the whole crazy idea. 'A—a few minutes ago I had a visitor…it was amazing she caught me here at the flat. My cousin Vivien's landed in town, from New York, where she's based these days. She's only here for a couple of days,' she went on breathlessly, 'and she's very anxious to meet Emma. She was always closer to Serena than to me.'

She paused, sucking in a much-needed breath. Carefully as she'd planned her story, it was filled with pitfalls.

'She's also keen to see Raeburns' Nest where Serena and Hamish used to live,' she rushed on, fearing that Cam might offer to drive the baby up to Sydney to meet Vivien. 'She could do with a restful break, she says.' She was warming to her theme. 'Cam, I realise this is terrible timing, with me stuck up here in Sydney for the next couple of days, but—but would you mind having Vivien at Raeburns' Nest for the next couple of nights?'

'Well, no, of course not.' Cam didn't even hesitate. 'I'm just sorry you won't be here with us.'

Oh, I'll be there, she thought with a guilty twinge. 'Thanks, Cam.' She rushed on before she could have second thoughts. 'Vivien's going to borrow my car and bring it back in two days time. Then I can come home.' *Home*… She felt a warm glow. She thought of Raeburns' Nest as home now, not this cold empty flat.

'Vivien's—um—just popped out to the corner shop to grab some rolls for lunch.' She didn't want Cam asking to speak to Vivien on the phone. She wanted him to *see* her first. 'She says she'll eat hers on the way to Raeburns' Nest…assuming she's welcome, of course.'

'You must tell her she's perfectly welcome,' Cam insisted, and asked, 'What's she like, this cousin of yours? I didn't even know you had a first cousin called Vivien. Was she at your sister's wedding?'

'No…she had other commitments. She's a—a photographic model.' She'd dreamed up the idea last night. 'A striking, dark-eyed brunette.' That should spark his interest, she thought with a stab of the old hurt. 'She's the daughter of my—my mother's older sister, who died when Vivien was a child.'

It was true that her mother had had an older sister who'd died of cancer at the age of thirty, but she'd died childless. 'Vivien was brought up in—in Queensland by her father, who remarried,' she improvised. 'I've only met her a couple of times before…and only once since she became a model. She tends to bowl into Australia and bowl out again.'

Was Cam already relishing the thought of meeting this jet-setting glamour puss?

She moved on to the more difficult part. 'We're

very alike, in a way…or so people say. Our features and build, maybe…but that's about all. We have totally different personalities.' She laughed, a brittle laugh. 'And she's a ravishing brunette—as dark as I'm fair.'

'Well…I'll look forward to meeting her. Anyone who looks like you, Roxy, must be worth meeting.'

Her heart gave a uneasy flutter. Would the raven-haired Roxy look-alike appeal to him more than the original blue-eyed blond Roxy? She frowned into Vivien's smouldering dark eyes. Was she making a big mistake putting temptation in Cam's path, in the very week leading up to his wedding day?

What if he tried to make a pass at Vivien?

But that was the idea! To see if he *would.*

'So it's all right if Vivien comes now…as soon as she comes back?' she asked quickly. 'She's really anxious to meet Emma, Cam. And you, of course,' she added sweetly, though the expression she saw in the mirror wasn't so sweet. Vivien was glowering back at her.

She huffed out a sigh. If Cam did end up succumbing to Vivien's sultry charms, then it would be best to know where she stood before her wedding day…best to know what she'd have to put up with if she went ahead with this marriage of convenience. She would have to decide then, once and for all, whether she could face up to having a philandering husband…and never revealing to him that she knew…never revealing the depth of her own feelings—for him.

She would have to...for her beloved niece's sake!

If nothing else—another sigh slipped from her—this would be a good test. A good test of Cam Raeburn's fidelity—and his commitment to his second marriage.

CHAPTER ELEVEN

CAM'S gaze, narrowed against the bright afternoon sun, swept over his dark-eyed houseguest as she swung her stocking-clad legs from the baby Mazda and rose slowly—sensuously, Roxy hoped—to face him. His eyes appeared to dwell for a moment on the rise and fall of her breasts under the slinky red dress, before flicking up to rest on her parted lips, just as she moistened them with a nervous flick of her tongue.

'Well...Roxy was right,' he drawled. 'There is a remarkable likeness.'

Remembering who she was meant to be, Roxy pouted, forming a peevish *moue* with her glossy red lips.

'People say there's a likeness, but I can't see it myself.' She'd remembered to lower her voice a notch, giving it a sultry huskiness. 'Roxy's a nice girl, but a bit drab, to be honest. And scruffy! Her hair's always a mess, she hardly ever bothers with make-up, not even lipstick half the time, and those clothes she wears! They do nothing for her at all.'

With a disdainful shake of her head, Roxy slid her hands down over her clinging red dress in a provocative gesture that amazed even herself. Where had it come from? It was so unlike her!

'I thought, after all this time, Roxy might have changed, but she hasn't.' She let her mascara-laden lashes flutter upwards, and smiled seductively at Cam.

'But that's Roxy. She doesn't care how she looks.'
She sighed, and added daringly, 'I could do wonders
for her if she'd only let me.'

'I think she's just perfect as she is,' Cam said
coolly.

Roxy's eyes flared in surprise, a warm tingle rip-
pling through her. Then remembering her role, she
gave a low chuckle and pulled a face.

'Oh, I daresay she'll make a perfect little wife and
mother. The capable, homespun, doting-mother type.
Reliable to a fault. And that's what you want, isn't it,
Cam? Roxy explained your situation...how you're
marrying each other to give your niece two loving
parents again, after the poor child's tragic loss.'

She saw a frown appear between his brows and
stopped breathing for a second. Was he already growing suspicious? Or was she fooling him far better than
she'd ever dreamed?

'You don't mind me staying a couple of nights, do
you, Cam?' She batted her eyelashes—hopefully
without overdoing it. 'I'm dying to meet the baby...'

'Emma's asleep at the moment.' Cam put emphasis
on the word 'Emma', as if to remind Roxy's cousin
that the baby did have a name. 'Mary, who baby-sits
for us, has just gone home—she looked after Emma
earlier today while I was at work. And yes, of course
you're welcome, Vivien...family are always welcome.' He gave a quick smile, sending a bittersweet
pang through Roxy, knowing it was for Vivien, not
for her.

'How about I show you to your room and get you
settled in?' Cam reached into the car's rear seat for
her bag. 'By then Emma might be awake.' As he

hauled the bag out he grimaced. 'Hell! What do you have in here? Bricks?'

Roxy gulped, flushing under Vivien's fake pink cheeks. She'd packed the books she'd bought that morning—three heavy tomes! Instead of leaving them at her flat to pick up after Vivien returned to Sydney in two days, she'd decided to bring them to Raeburns' Nest with her as insurance in case—heaven forbid— she was unmasked. She could show them to Cam and hope that her plan for the future might appease him a little.

She lifted her chin. Vivien's chin. 'It's just shoes…and make-up and stuff,' she said with a slight sniff, implying that models needed such things. 'You're not saying it's too heavy for you, are you, Cam?' she taunted softly. 'A powerful hunk like you?'

Cam merely smiled and turned towards the house. As she followed him—to be on the safe side she'd worn red pumps with a broad heel, avoiding tricky stiletto heels—she said gushingly, in her new sultry voice, 'I expect to earn my keep while I'm here…'

Cam glanced round with raised eyebrows.

She smiled brightly. 'If you'll show me what to do, Cam, I'll look after your niece while you're at work tomorrow.' She didn't want him asking Mary to come back in the morning now that she—Roxy—was home to take care of their niece.

'That's why I'm staying here for a couple of nights, after all…to help you with the baby. One of the reasons,' she added in a beguiling purr, running her gaze over Cam the way he'd run his over her.

But he'd already turned away. 'And to get to know Emma, of course,' she added hastily, not wanting him to think that she didn't care about the baby…or

couldn't be trusted with her. 'I adore babies. I just
know I'm going to love little Emma. But I draw a
line at changing dirty diapers and getting up in the
night—I need my beauty sleep.'

She couldn't have Cam seeing her in the middle of
the night without her make-up, wig, and contact
lenses!

'My looks are my livelihood,' she explained with
a tinkling little laugh. 'I'm a model.'

'Yes, Roxy told me.' Cam glanced round, his brow
lifting. 'I thought models had to be tall and skinny as
beanpoles?'

Roxy's heart missed a beat. In the past month she'd
regained her lost weight and added new curves. She
was far too shapely—and too petite—to be a catwalk
model! She jerked out, 'I'm a photographic model.
Face shots, mostly.'

'Well, you certainly have the face for it,' Cam said,
and she didn't know whether to be flattered or hurt.
Vivien was a dark-eyed brunette, after all. Cam was
partial to dark-eyed brunettes. Was he *still* partial to
them? she wondered with a trembling sigh. Maybe,
as the vampish Vivien, she would find out.

Cam opened the side door of the house and waved
her in, brushing her arm with his hand as he stepped
in after her and steered her towards the passage.

Roxy trembled at his touch. But he wasn't touching
her...he was touching Vivien.

'I'll lead the way, shall I?' Cam eased past her.
Halfway along the passage Roxy held her breath, hoping he wasn't planning to put Vivien into the small
den that she—Roxy—had taken over, opposite his
own room and the nursery. It had no en suite, and she
had no wish to risk running into Cam without her

black wig, brown contact lenses or dramatic face make-up. She could hardly wear them to bed!

If he did try to put her in there, she would just have to pretend that a crying baby in the night would disturb her precious beauty sleep, and demand another room as far away as possible.

To her relief, he sailed straight past the den. The door to his own room, directly opposite, lay open, she noticed as she glanced round. She could see the big king-size bed.

'Your room, Cam?' she purred, slowing her steps. 'The room you already share with Roxy, no doubt,' she added provocatively—wondering at her own temerity. What was she trying to do? Taunt Cam into admitting that they hadn't yet slept together? Drive Cam, in his frustration, into another woman's arms? Into *Vivien's* arms?

'Not for the next couple of nights, unfortunately,' Cam said smoothly.

Roxy swallowed a lump in her throat. Cam was implying that he was already sleeping with his bride-to-be...and that he was sorry she wouldn't be in his bed for the next two nights. *Unfortunately,* he'd said. And he'd said it without tossing any rakish, meaningful glances at Vivien.

Her eyes misted—not just at his unexpected show of loyalty, but because they were now passing the nursery where her beloved Emma lay peacefully sleeping.

Was her baby niece missing her?

Her arms were aching to hold Emma again, to see the baby's heartmelting smiles again, but she contained her impatience while Cam settled her into the guest wing—at a safe distance from the master bedroom and that big bed. It suited her perfectly. Having an en suite, she could shut herself in here at night and not appear again until she was fully wigged and made up as cousin Vivien!

'Roxy sounded a bit edgy on the phone,' Cam commented before leaving her to unpack. 'Did she seem...happy, Vivien? She's giving up a lot to move down here and become a full-time wife and mother.'

'Happy?' Roxy moved to the window to look out over the cliffs, carefully averting her gaze, to avoid his. She would be ecstatically happy...if she only knew that her husband-to-be was going to remain committed to his marriage...to *her*.

Her eyes misted again, and she blinked. Vivien wouldn't be misty-eyed. She wasn't the misty-eyed type. 'She was perfectly happy to give up her field work, she told me.' She paused, flicking her tongue over her scarlet lips. 'All my cousin wants is to be a full-time wife and mother.' She swung round—languidly. 'If she seemed edgy it was probably because she's upset about being away from her baby niece. She said it was agony being away from Emma, even for a few hours—let alone a couple of days.'

'Only from Emma?' Cam asked with a wry smile.

Roxy felt a flush rising and whirled away before he could catch it. Vivien wouldn't flush, either!

'Oh, what a lovely bathroom!' she cried as she flung open the door of the adjoining en suite. 'I can see I'm going to be very comfortable here.' Vivien would be the type who would notice bathrooms and spend long hours there.

'Well, I'll leave you to unpack and freshen up.' Cam began to leave, then paused. 'I'll make you a cup of tea. Or would you rather have coffee? Or a cool drink?'

She flashed him a dazzling smile—and felt his eyes on her glossy red lips. Her answer, low and sultry as it was, held a faint tremor.

'A cool drink sounds divine…but something soft, thanks, Cam. I'd better not breathe alcohol over your niece. Maybe at dinner?' she cooed, valiantly dredging up that seductive purr again. 'Who cooks your dinner, by the way, while Roxy's away?'

She raised innocent eyes to his—and felt her heart leap as they came into contact with a gaze as dark as Vivien's. Darker. 'I can't cook to save myself, I'm afraid.' She waved a careless hand. 'I'm used to eating out.'

She could hardly offer to cook for him. It wouldn't do for Cam to see her cooking the same dishes Roxy had prepared for him! She'd already exhausted her meagre repertoire.

'Don't worry, I can cook,' Cam assured her. 'But I won't have to tonight…Philomena's cooked us her famous moussaka. We just have to heat it up when we're ready.'

Roxy remembered to inquire, 'Philomena? Who is she?'

'She's our saviour,' Cam said with a smile—a smile that shivered through her veins. 'She's an amazingly energetic mother of six who comes in to clean and tidy up after us.'

Roxy swallowed. *Our* saviour, he'd said. Meaning Roxy and his? Was he thinking of them both as a couple now?

Unless 'our' meant Cam and his niece.

She chewed on her painted lip as Cam strode from the room.

*   *   *

Emma woke crying.

'The baby's awake.' Roxy jumped up, then paused, remembering who she was supposed to be. Would the sophisticated Vivian be this eager to rush to a baby?

I don't care what Cam thinks, she decided recklessly. She couldn't wait a second longer to see Emma. At his nod she hurried from the room, realising as she reached the passage that Cam was at her heels. Realising, too—just in time—that Vivien wouldn't know where the nursery was. The door had been shut earlier and Cam hadn't pointed it out to her.

'Which room?' she asked with a waggle of her hand, setting her gold bracelets jingling. She'd brought her most outlandish jewellery with her, along with any showy clothes she could find. 'Don't worry, I can hear her.' Pretending that the baby's cries were showing her the way, she yanked open the nursery door.

'Better let me go in first,' Cam said, touching her arm. 'She's a bit shy with strangers.'

Strangers. That brought her up abruptly. Would Emma see her as a stranger, all over again? Her heart dived to her bright red shoes.

No, she thought, rallying. Emma will know me...even if Cam doesn't. Cam was *expecting* a look-alike cousin, but Emma's expecting to see Roxy. Black hair and dark eyes won't fool Emma.

She hoped.

She watched Cam lean over the cot and pick up the baby. The familiar sight of this huge man showing such tenderness and care for a small baby brought the usual catch to her throat. Emma stopped crying instantly, and smiled up at him. Cam talked to her for a moment in a conversational way, until she began gurgling and laughing, and Roxy wondered anew at the bond between Cam and his niece. They were as close now as any father and daughter.

Did Emma feel as close to *her?* As close as she had felt to her mother? Roxy blinked away a prickle of tears. She couldn't wait another second.

'Emma...' she cooed, remembering to use Vivien's sultry purr as she closed the gap between them. 'Well, now...aren't you a sweetie?' She held out her arms. 'Want to come to your...Aunt Vivien?' The name almost stuck in her throat.

For a scary second Emma just stared at her. Then she smiled her gorgeous smile and held out her arms.

With a rush of relief, Roxy gathered the baby in her arms, drinking in the sweet baby scent of her, the warm cuddly softness. For a few delirious seconds she forgot everything but the joy of holding her niece, of being warmly accepted, welcomed back, recognised. Because surely this ready acceptance meant that Emma must have recognised her?

She remembered Cam, realised he was watching her intently, and with some amazement, and turned to him with a careless laugh. 'Now what do I do? Does she need feeding? Or what?' The vampish Vivien was supposed to be more temptress, she reminded herself, than mother-figure!

'She might want a drink and something to nibble,' Cam said, stepping over to take Emma from her. Roxy reluctantly handed her over. 'Then she usually likes a bit of exercise—she's just learning to crawl,' he told her. 'Or she'll play with her toys. A walk's out this afternoon, I'm afraid—it's just started to rain.'

Roxy glanced towards the window. 'Well, so it has.

Where did the sun go? Never mind, I'm not an out-doorsy person,' she said lightly, wanting to stress the differences between Vivien and Roxy.

She was relieved that the summery warmth of the past few days had given way to rain and cooler con-ditions. She could hardly go swimming in a wig and full make-up! As an added precaution she was trying to hide Roxy's natural tan—which meant sticking to long sleeves, panty hose and heavy make-up.

She thanked her lucky stars that they weren't in the midst of a December heat wave!

Somehow she survived the rest of that long after-noon. Baby Emma, needing constant attention, helped to ease some of Roxy's tension. She concentrated happily on her niece—even though, with Cam around, she had to pretend that she knew little about caring for babies and would be only too ready to hand Emma back the instant she became difficult or demanding.

It was an ordeal keeping up the pretence, but it would only be for one more day, Roxy consoled her-self.

And two nights.

She dragged in a shaky breath. The evenings would be the test, the real torture. The evenings, alone with Cam.

And this evening was almost here.

CHAPTER TWELVE

THE wind had picked up and the rain was falling steadily now, drumming down on the roof and thudding against the windows. The temperature was tumbling.

'Well,' Cam commented, 'our early burst of summer appears to have been an illusion. We're back to winter with a vengeance.'

They were sitting at the dining-room table—just the two of them, now that Emma was in bed asleep—enjoying Philomena's delicious moussaka, with a fresh green salad, crusty bread rolls and a bottle of burgundy.

'Seems like it,' Roxy agreed in her new husky voice. She shook her head as Cam offered more wine, her hands shaking as she put down her empty glass. Fielding Cam's questions over dinner, and having to watch what she said the whole time, was nerve-racking. 'I'll just go and...' For a mad second she was tempted to say, *Slip into something more comfortable,* but she didn't want to push her luck. 'Change into something warmer.'

She was dying to get out of this clinging red dress and the hard-soled red pumps. How could anyone relax in clothes like these?

'I'll get the apple pie,' Cam offered, rising as she did. 'Like ice-cream with it? Or whipped cream? Or both?'

Roxy feigned a shudder. 'I'll just have coffee, thanks. I mustn't put on any weight. My looks are my—'

'Livelihood?' Cam provided with an amused glimmer in his eye, his lip quirking in a way that was nearly Roxy's undoing.

She felt a giggle rising and only just managed to stifle it. Vivien wouldn't be amused. As she tossed her head and swept off to her room, she wondered if she and Cam would laugh about all this one day…in the distant future, when she considered it safe to tell him. If she ever did.

If he didn't unmask her in the meantime!

She peeked in on Emma on her way to the guest wing. The baby was fast asleep, breathing evenly, her small chest rising and falling. Roxy felt a loving warmth surging through her, but managed to resist the impulse to lean over the cot and touch her niece. She was Vivien, she had to remember. Vivien wouldn't be so sentimental. Or so caring.

Back in her room, she thankfully kicked off her red shoes and peeled off the slinky red dress, pulling on a sweater and a pair of dressy black slacks that she'd brought from her Sydney flat, and slipping her feet into comfortable black slipons that Cam hadn't yet seen. She spent a few more minutes touching up her lipstick, powdering her nose and readjusting her black wig. She added a bit more mascara and eye shadow for good measure.

As she headed back to rejoin Cam she resolved to make her excuses the moment she'd had her coffee, and then retire for the night. Cam wouldn't question

it. She'd already told him she needed her beauty
sleep.

She grinned impishly as she hastened along the
passage to the dining room. So far things were going
brilliantly. Cam didn't suspect a thing. She could even
dare to be a bit adventurous, perhaps. Use Vivien's
feminine wiles to find out just how susceptible Cam
was to flirtatious dark-eyed brunettes.

She had to wipe the mischievous smile from her
lips before she stepped into the dining room.

'In here,' Cam called from the family room. 'It's
cosier in here.'

Cosier? The hairs rose at Roxy's nape. Did he
mean that the armchairs were more comfortable? Or
was he setting a mood? Was seduction already on his
mind?

Her old mistrust of him warred with amused irony
at the idea of him making a pass at a woman who
didn't even exist! What would she do if he did try
anything? Her heart wavered. Suddenly she didn't
feel so wickedly impish any more.

She entered the family room warily, to find Cam
lounging on the sofa. As she sank into an armchair-
not giving him a chance to wave her to the sofa beside
him—he rose to pour her a cup of coffee from the
pot he'd brought in.

She smiled brightly—valiantly—gathering her
strength to field off more questions about Vivien's
glamorous life and background. But the first person
Cam mentioned was Roxy!

'I thought Roxy might have rung by now,' he commented as he set her coffee down beside her and took
his own back to the sofa.

Roxy's heart shrivelled a little. Did he think that she—Roxy—didn't care enough about her baby niece to call and check up on her?

'She's only been away from Emma for one day, Cam,' she reminded him in Vivien's husky drawl. 'Not even that. She saw Emma this morning at breakfast.'

She could have bitten her tongue out as Cam looked up sharply, as if wondering how Vivien could possibly know that.

'Roxy said she left here straight after breakfast,' she said with a shrug. 'Look, I'm sure she'll call you in the morning, Cam. She's crazy about that kid. It's why she was so relieved that I could be here with the baby while she's seeing agents and running around doing all the things one does before a wedding.'

But this wasn't a *real* wedding. She didn't need to do a thing! She didn't even intend to buy a new dress. She planned to wear the blue silk dress she'd worn to Serena's wedding. It had caught Cam's eye then—maybe it would again, if there were no gorgeous brunettes to overshadow her.

'And it's thoughtful of you to come, Vivien,' Cam acknowledged, his eyes warm—but thankfully, as far as she could see, with no seductive messages in them. 'But it wasn't Roxy's concern for Emma that I was thinking about,' he added with a swift frown. 'I just thought she would have called to let me know how the agent's visit went. But she's probably out with friends.'

Roxy swallowed. There was a brooding note in his voice. Was he afraid she might enjoy herself so much that she wouldn't want to come back? Or was he actually *missing* her? After only a few hours?

She took a careful breath and said, in Vivien's low, husky drawl, 'You're not worried, are you, Cam, that Roxy might change her mind and want to take up her archeological career again?' She eyed him for a tense moment before adding, 'She told me how you'd made it a condition of your marriage that she gave up her field work.'

His dark eyes sharpened under his heavy brows. 'Roxy seems to have told you a lot in a very short time.'

Roxy tried not to panic. 'We're family,' she said as coolly as she could. 'Roxy wanted to put me in the picture before I…met you. So I'd know what to expect.' She jerked a careless shoulder. Vivien would be bored talking about another woman. But reassuring Cam was more important than Vivien right now.

'You have no need to worry, you know,' she assured him throatily. 'Roxy's not the type to back out of a deal. Anyway, she doesn't want to. She says she's given up her career because *she* wants to, not because *you* want her to. She won't be like me, Cam…wanting to flit off hither and yon all the time.'

She paused, lifting a heavily pencilled eyebrow. 'I take it you're against career wives, Cam? Career wives who travel.'

Cam's brow knitted again. 'I don't have anything against a woman having a career…but if the absences are lengthy, or if the wife feels frustrated at home, it's the children who suffer most.'

Roxy cleared her throat. 'You sound as if you're speaking from experience, Cam,' she murmured, her heart picking up a beat at the way he was opening up to Vivien. 'I thought you had no children from your first marriage?'

Cam's dark eyes pierced hers, as if he was wondering how she would know about his first marriage.

She gulped, explaining quickly, 'Roxy mentioned it. You didn't, did you? Have children?'

Cam shook his head, a lock of dark hair slipping over his brow, giving her an intense urge to reach out and flick it back.

'My wife decided that her high-powered law career and a dazzling offer from an international merchant bank, based in New York, were more important than the children she'd pretended to want before we got married. She did offer—grudgingly—to have my children, on condition that I bring them up myself, back here in Australia. She didn't want to be bothered with their upbringing. When I refused to play ball she filed for divorce and ran off to New York with one of her equally ambitious legal colleagues. They're married now. And blissfully childless.'

His brow lowered, shadowing his eyes. 'I had no wish to bring up children on my own...the way my brother and I were brought up by our father after *our* mother shot through. I wouldn't have wished that kind of life on any child...being rejected, raised without a mother, looked after by strangers, shunted off to relatives and boarding school...feeling unwanted and unloved.'

Roxy tried not to show how affected she was by his story. Vivien wouldn't be showing any reaction, she thought, wishing she could scrub the self-centered Vivien and show her real feelings. She was longing to hold out her arms to him and offer him comfort for the grievous hurts of the past. His mother *and* his ex-wife…neither wanting to devote any time to their children, neither willing to give love or comfort. It explained so much.

'*Why* did your mother leave you?' she breathed, forgetting for a second that Vivien wasn't likely to be interested in Cam Raeburn's mother. But Roxy needed to know, and Cam mightn't open up like this again. Had his mother been a career-driven woman like his ex-wife, Kimberley? Like she—his soon-to-be second wife—had been at the time he'd proposed to her? And might want to be again, for all Cam knew.

He gave a shrug, as if it no longer mattered to him. 'My mother was a frustrated actress. A former soapie star. She left us to try to resurrect her acting career. Not here in Australia, which Dad might have accepted, but in Hollywood. He had no intention of bringing up his sons in Hollywood. Not that my mother wanted us around anyway, getting in her way, making her feel old. She quickly and conveniently forgot that we even existed.'

Roxy's heart went out to him. But she was Vivien, she had to remember.

'Hollywood!' Vivien would be impressed with that. 'Was she well-known?'

'Sadly for her, no.' Cam's mouth twisted. 'She only ever landed bit parts. Dad kept hoping she'd get it out of her system and come home, even if only for a visit, but she never did. The frustration and disappointment of never making it big time killed her in the end. She took to drugs and alcohol and eventually overdosed. She died alone in a shabby boarding house.'

Roxy forgot to hide her shock this time. 'How awful!' She gulped, quickly composing herself. 'So…you never saw your mother again, after she walked out on you?'

'Never saw her or heard from her. I guess she didn't want to admit to anyone in Hollywood that she had two growing boys.'

'How old were you when she died?'

'Thirteen. I was five when she left home, my brother three.'

Roxy's heart bled for the two little boys who'd lost their mother at the tender age of five and three. If boys needed their mothers, Cam seemed to be saying, little girls must surely need them even more.

'No wonder you're so anxious for Emma to have a mother, Cam.' Unable to prevent it, Roxy's eyes filled with tears…for the unloved little boy he'd once been, for the motherless Emma, for her beloved sister, Serena, and perhaps for herself, too, in love with a man who didn't love *her*.

She blinked—then remembering that she was wearing loads of mascara and eyeliner, she grabbed a tissue and dabbed at her eyes, hoping she didn't already look a complete mess.

'Sorry, Cam,' she wavered. 'I'm not normally the blubbery type.'

Cam smiled, his face crinkling in that familiar, heart-stopping way. But he was smiling at Vivien, not at her.

'You're a sympathetic woman, Vivien. Easy to talk to. You tend to draw things out of me.' Cam's smile turned rueful. His eyes had a musing, faraway look that brought a faint frown to Roxy's brow. Was he regretting, suddenly, that he was engaged to another woman? Wishing he'd chosen this sympathetic, *dark-eyed brunette* instead?

She felt a quiver of unease. And—it was bizarre— a stab of jealousy. She was jealous of the woman she was pretending to be!

She didn't want Cam falling for the flashy brunette—the nonexistent cousin—she'd sent here in her place! She wanted Cam to have eyes for no other woman but herself!

'You remind me of Roxy in a way...not just in looks.' Cam was sitting back now, eyeing her speculatively.

A chill feathered down Roxy's spine. 'In *what* way?' she demanded with a pout. Vivien wouldn't want to be like Roxy, she thought. Unless... Her heart caught in midbeat. Did she attract him *physically?* Was that what he meant?

Her whole body tensed, her spirits tumbling. The way he was looking at her... He'd be kissing her next!

Alarmed, she cast around for a way of escape, forgetting that she'd wanted to tempt him to find out what he'd be likely to do.

She jerked her head round. 'I think I heard Emma... No, Cam, let me go and check.' She waved him back and rose quickly. 'I'll settle her down...or cover her up if she needs it. And then, if you don't mind, Cam, I think I'll go to bed.'

She realised she sounded breathless—*vamps, you idiot, don't get breathless*—and slowed herself down, injecting a cooler, huskier note. 'It's been a long day and I need my—' she paused…deliberately this time. She couldn't resist it.

'Beauty sleep?' Cam suggest, grinning lopsidedly up at her.

She curbed her own rising laughter, jutting out her chin as Vivien would do if she suspected someone was making fun of her.

Not daring to meet his eye, she fled.

CHAPTER THIRTEEN

SAFELY back in her bedroom after checking on Emma—who hadn't made a peep and was still sleeping soundly—she leaned against her door, breathing heavily, her heart skittering. Should she have stayed to find out if Cam actually *would* have kissed her?

She licked dry lips. Now she would never know.

But there would be other opportunities. Vivien still had one more night here at Raeburns' Nest. One more full day and night to flutter her eyelashes at Cam and flirt outrageously to see if he would weaken under her wiles and succumb to temptation.

Or would she chicken out again?

Being here at Raeburns' Nest, so close to him, close enough to touch him, close enough to see every change of expression, was both rapture and torment. Roxy closed her eyes and pictured his face…the sexy curved smile, the coal-dark glitter of his eyes, the deeply etched lines slashing his cheeks to his jawline. If only she didn't want to kiss *him* so badly!

Thinking of his kisses—the intoxicating warmth of his lips, the hungry rasp of his breath, her own aching response—made her heart beat even faster, her skin break out in prickly beads of sweat.

Was he missing Roxy at all? She groaned. Forcing her body to move, she dragged herself to the en suite to begin the laborious task of removing her make-up, contact lenses and teased black wig.

Knowing she'd have trouble sleeping, she read for a while before switching off her bedside lamp. It didn't help. For the next couple of hours she tossed about in her bed, trying vainly to sleep—at the same time listening for the slightest sound, wondering what she'd do if she heard furtive footsteps approaching and a tap at her door. It had no lock or key, and she felt nerve-tinglingly vulnerable.

She had two worries—the worry of Cam seeing her without her vampish disguise…and the heart-sickening fear that he might succumb to an irresistible urge to seduce Vivien during the night, right here in the guest room's double bed!

In the end she hauled herself out of bed and jammed a wedge-shaped doorstop under the door. Cam might still come to her bedroom and knock, hoping Vivien would welcome him into her room and her bed, but at least he wouldn't be able to bowl straight in, unannounced!

But Cam didn't knock and he didn't try to bowl straight in, and eventually she stopped listening for him and fell into a restless sleep.

In the morning, she took a reviving shower—Vivien, she reasoned, would be unlikely to make an early appearance, so she took her time. Then she went through the whole arduous beautification process again…carefully applying make-up, blusher and glossy red lipstick, enhancing her eyes with black eyeliner, smudgy blue eye shadow and oodles of black mascara, thickening and darkening her eyebrows with a heavy black pencil, then carefully masking her blue eyes with the bold dark-brown contact lenses.

Since it still looked cool and overcast outside, she pulled on a pair of black leggings and a body-hugging tiger-print sweater, avoiding the pants and sweater she'd worn the night before—Vivien would be unlikely to wear the same thing twice.

She thrust her feet into black walking shoes, knowing she'd have to go out later this morning to find a public phone to give Cam a call at work. He'd be expecting a call from Roxy, and she didn't want to risk calling him from the house. Philomena might overhear her—or his telephone bill, when it came, might give her away.

Finally she pulled on the black wig and teased it into shape, and as a flamboyant final touch, she added a pair of dangly earrings.

She surveyed the result in the mirror and nodded, satisfied—even as her heartbeat resumed its nervous, erratic thudding.

Vivien was ready to face battle again. Ready to face Cam again.

Before leaving the room she remembered to give herself a dab of perfume, choosing a heady French perfume that Blanche had given her. She hadn't worn it before—she preferred lighter floral fragrances—but on Vivien it was perfect.

'Well, Vivien…what are you waiting for?' She was ready for breakfast—more than ready. Normally she had it much earlier than this.

Both the nursery and Cam's master bedroom appeared deserted as she passed them by—with a wiggle of her hips in case Cam was watching, throwing herself into the vampish role she'd cast for herself. The role she was already half regretting.

She'd plunged into it for her own peace of mind, but what peace of mind was she going to have if Cam succumbed to Vivien's sultry-eyed charms? It would break her heart. But at least she would know what kind of husband she was marrying—and could guard her heart in the future.

Cam was in the kitchen with the baby, patiently feeding his niece her breakfast. Roxy's breath caught at the sight of him, so tall and rawboned and sexy, with a wayward lock of dark hair flopping across his brow and an air of deep concentration on his face as he smilingly offered the baby encouragement.

She swallowed and moved forward, faltering as she realised Cam was wearing casual jeans and a sweater. Wasn't he going to work today?

'Good morning,' she said brightly, remembering just in time to lower her voice a decibel. 'Hi there, baby Emma,' she cooed, flashing Vivien's brilliant smile—resisting the impulse to run forward and snatch her up. 'Well, what a good little girl you are. You've eaten up all your breakfast!'

Cam glanced round, his gaze doing a lazy sweep over her. With a flutter of unease, Roxy wondered if it was an appreciative look…or a critical one. Or simply a coolly assessing look? Assessing her for what, though?

She bravely flashed another dazzling smile, trying not to feel self-conscious—as she always tended to in this sweater, which was why she'd left it at her flat in town when she'd first come to Raeburns' Nest. Like the clinging red dress and the red pumps, she'd only ever worn the top once before. They just weren't Roxy-type clothes.

Which made them perfect. She wasn't meant to *be* Roxy!

'Well…you look as if you're ready for a modelling assignment rather than a bout of baby-sitting,' Cam drawled, his gaze coming to rest on her carefully made-up face. 'Or are you going out somewhere?'

Roxy hesitated, her mind racing ahead. If Cam intended to stay at home all day with Vivien and his baby niece, how was she—Roxy—going to have a chance to slip out and call him on the phone? There were no phone boxes nearby, as far as she knew.

Cam's question about going out gave her the solution.

'Well,' she murmured in Vivien's sultry purr, 'if you're going to be at home today, Cam, I might grab the chance to pop out for a while. I need to find a…a pharmacy,' she plucked from the air. '*Are* you staying at home?'

She saw something flicker in his eyes, and wasn't sure if it was anticipation at the thought of being at home all day, close to Vivien, or amusement that his dark-eyed guest was seizing her chance to get out of the house—and away from the baby!

'I'll be home all morning and for lunch, but I might pop up to the plant this afternoon.' Cam paused, the edge of his mouth lifting in a whimsical smile. 'I wouldn't leave you here to baby-sit alone for the whole day…'

'But I'm *happy* to baby-sit,' she protested. If he didn't hear from her—from *Roxy*—this morning, he'd think she didn't care about Emma…or about him. She couldn't wait until this afternoon to call him. It would seem like an afterthought.

'That's why I'm here, remember?' she persisted. 'To spend time with my baby cousin.' She hid her desperation under a flutter of Vivien's black lashes. 'I don't really need to go out, Cam. I can go later, if you want to go to work this morning. All day, I mean.'

As he eyed her in faint surprise, she appealed to him with Vivien's bold dark eyes. 'I'd *like* to look after Emma,' she purred. She could take the baby in the car with her to find a phone box—after Cam had gone.

His eyes held hers for a long, breath-stopping moment. Was he wondering if he could trust Roxy's flighty cousin with his baby niece for the whole day? Or was he seeing Vivien in a new light? As responsible as well as caring?

'That's kind of you, Vivien. I appreciate it…but I think you'll find that an afternoon alone with a lively baby will be quite long enough. As for this morning, we'll *all* go out,' he decided, to Roxy's horror. 'I'll drive you into Kiama, Vivien, and you can go to the pharmacy while I pop into the supermarket with Emma. We've run out of a few things.'

Roxy could do nothing but shrug, as if the arrangement was fine by her. But inwardly she was tearing her hair. How could she call Cam—as Roxy—if he came to Kiama with her?

She'd just have to call him from the pharmacy, while he was at the supermarket. He'd have his mobile phone with him—he'd told Roxy he would keep it on, wherever he was.

'Afterwards I'll show you Kiama's famous Blow-hole,' Cam rattled on, 'and then take you for a drive down the coast…it's very scenic. Emma loves travelling in the car. She'll probably go to sleep. Now, Vivien…what would you like for breakfast?' he asked, wiping Emma's face and lifting her out of her highchair.

Roxy almost said automatically, 'Fruit and muesli,' her usual breakfast, but remembered in time that she was meant to be Vivien. Choosing the same breakfast just might be too much of a coincidence. She found a way around it. 'Oh, I'm not fussy. I'll have what Roxy normally has.'

Cam pointed to a bowl of fresh fruit on the table. 'Roxy normally has fresh fruit and muesli, followed by toast. Help yourself. The muesli, milk and butter are in the fridge, bread's on the bench. Help yourself. Will you have tea? Coffee?'

Because Roxy normally had tea for breakfast, she chose coffee.

As she was sipping it the phone rang. Cam grabbed it. 'Roxy? No, I'm sorry, professor, she's… Oh, yes, sure.' He was silent for a moment, listening.

Roxy had turned to stone. *Professor?* Professor *Bergman?* Had the professor received her letter already? Was he calling to try to change her mind, refusing to accept no for an answer? Why else would be call her personally?

'Right…yes, I will. Thank you, professor.' Cam hung up. He was looking a bit shell-shocked, Roxy thought, gulping. As well he might, if the professor was being persistent.

'Anything wrong?' she asked in Vivien's husky voice. She hardly had to put it on!

Cam gave a start, as if he'd forgotten she was there.

He must be worried sick, Roxy brooded, that I'll accept the professor's offer the second time around. Or that I'll refuse it and be miserable. Or won't he even tell me about the call?

He hadn't given the professor her phone number in Sydney, she'd noted.

If only she could reassure him! But she couldn't! She couldn't say a single word. She would just have to wait until she rang him later, and see if he mentioned it then. And reassure him when he did. *If* he did.

An hour later they were on their way to Kiama in Cam's station wagon, Emma sitting perkily in her car seat in the back. Roxy's palms were sweating. It was vital that Cam didn't come with her to the pharmacy.

She just hoped he'd remembered to bring his mobile phone with him-and had kept it switched on!

As Cam drove through the small coastal town she cried, 'There's a pharmacy!' It was one she'd never been into—as Roxy. And a safe distance from the supermarket. 'Just drop me off here, Cam, and pick me up on your way back.'

But Cam kept on driving. 'There's a pharmacy at the supermarket shopping centre. It's just outside the town.'

Roxy gritted her teeth. She'd wanted to avoid that particular pharmacy. She was known there. It was Hamish's old pharmacy, which she'd used a few times since she'd been at Raeburns' Nest. How could she introduce herself as Roxy's cousin Vivien, ask to use their phone, and then call Cam as Roxy? *'Hi, Cam, Roxy here.'* Even if she didn't use her own name, she'd have to use her own voice—a voice

they were bound to recognise. They might see
through her disguise and say something later to Cam.

Why on earth had she told him she wanted to find
a *pharmacy?*

Swinging into the supermarket car park, Cam nosed
his car into a vacant parking spot.

'I'll take Emma,' he offered as he unbuckled the
baby and lifted her out. 'I'll show you where the pharmacy is, Vivien, and when I've finished at the supermarket I'll meet you back there. I shouldn't be
long…we don't need much.'

Roxy swallowed hard as she strode along beside
him, remembering to roll her hips each time he
glanced round. I'll have to find another phone quick
smart, she thought. Cam never wastes any time when
he shops. And if he only wants a few things… As
they entered the small complex, Cam waved a hand.
'There you are, Vivien.' The pharmacy lay on their
right. The supermarket was visible a few doors further
on, past a newsagent and a beauty salon.

Roxy's eyes gleamed. A beauty salon! 'No need to
rush, Cam,' she said airily. 'I—um—I need a prescription made up.' She flashed a smile at Emma. 'See
you, kid.' She paused to watch them go, pretending
to be inspecting the pharmacy window display, lingering in the doorway until she saw them disappear
inside the supermarket.

Then she made a dive for the one place she'd never
been before as Roxy. Why hadn't she thought of a
beauty salon in the first place? To the image-obsessed
Vivien, a beauty salon would be like a second home!

She breezed in and pranced up to the red-haired
receptionist. 'May I make an appointment please?'

She spoke in her normal voice, knowing she'd have to use her own voice shortly, to speak to Cam on the phone. 'For a trim and blowdry?' She could always call later and cancel it.

'Sure…when would you like it?' The receptionist glanced up at Vivien's mass of glossy black hair. Roxy wondered if she could tell it was a wig. Not that it mattered. Plenty of women—especially photographic models—must wear wigs on a bad hair day.

She opened her mouth to say 'Friday', and stopped. This coming Saturday, she recalled, was her wedding day! Why make an appointment for Vivien, when she—Roxy—was getting married at the weekend and could do with a special hairdo herself? Her short, choppy-layered bob had grown in the past month and was badly in need of a decent cut.

She let her eyes stray past the young receptionist to the tall, capable-looking hairdresser, who was primping the hair of a smartly dressed woman with wavy dark hair. Yes…why shouldn't *she* be pampered for once? It might be a low-key wedding, but she didn't have to get married looking like a scarecrow!

'Your name, please?'

Roxy turned back to her receptionist. 'Oh, it's not for me…it's for my cousin Roxy Warren. She's getting married on Saturday.'

'Oh. Right. Is 9:00 a.m. too early?'

Too early for Vivien perhaps, but not for Roxy. 'No, that's perfect. Thanks.'

'Right…we'll see you at 9:00 a.m. on Saturday then.' The girl smiled, showing small perfect teeth.

Roxy thanked her and pretended to leave, then paused. 'Oh, dear, I was meant to give someone a call. I don't suppose I could use your phone for a moment, could I?'

'Sure.' The girl pushed the phone towards her. 'Just dial O, then the number.'

'Um…it's a mobile phone number. Is that okay?' Roxy smiled Vivien's brilliant red smile.

'Sure.' The receptionist reached for a bottle of nail varnish.

Roxy took a deep breath. It was obvious the girl wasn't going to move away and let her speak in private. Never mind. She'd just have to be careful. She dialled Cam's mobile phone number, which she knew by heart, and held her breath until she heard the ringing tone she'd hoped to hear. He'd kept his phone switched on!

Hoping for a call from Roxy?

She felt her heart quickening—only to frown a second later. Why wasn't he answering? Had he left the phone in his car? Or at home?

Just as she was beginning to give up hope she heard a click. 'Cam Raeburn.'

Relief whooshed through her. 'Cam, it's me.' She could hardly say 'Roxy' with the receptionist listening in. She'd just told the girl that 'Roxy' was her cousin. 'How's—'

'Roxy! How are you? Not overdoing things I hope?'

Roxy gulped down a lump in her throat. He sounded genuinely pleased to hear from her, genuinely concerned about her. She felt a stab of guilt. If he knew that she was here in the shopping centre…that she was Vivien.

She shivered at the hazardous game she was playing.

'No, I'm fine,' she forced out. If Cam was upset about Professor Bergman's phone call, he wasn't showing it. Would he mention it? Or had he decided not to, not wanting her to be tempted all over again? She bit her lip, her heart going out to him.

'The agent's confident of a quick sale,' she said truthfully, adding in a breathless rush—not so truthfully, 'I've decided to go out this afternoon when he takes the prospective buyers through. I—I want to do some more shopping, and then I'll be meeting up with a couple of girlfriends and staying with one of them overnight.' She was deliberately vague, in case Cam asked for a phone number.

'I'll be on my way home in the morning as soon as—' she decided it was safe to say 'Vivien', since she hadn't given the receptionist her name '—as Vivien arrives back here with my car. I can hardly wait to come home,' she added with feeling. *Above all, I can't wait to dispense with the vampish Vivien.* 'Um…how's my cousin getting on?' she remembered to ask.

'Vivien? Fine.' There was a lot of background noise. Roxy had to strain to hear him. 'She and Emma get along like a house on fire.'

Because she knows it's me, Roxy longed to tell him.

'And what about you, Cam?' she couldn't resist asking. 'How are you getting along with my… delectable cousin? She's a bit of a dish, isn't she?' She found she was holding her breath again.

'Mmm…we're getting along fine, too,' Cam said without elaborating. A baby started crying. It sounded like Emma. 'Look, I'll have to go, Roxy. I'm at the supermarket checkout and Emma's playing up and Vivien's not here at the moment and they want my money. Look forward to seeing you tomorrow.'

The line went dead before Roxy had a chance to ask how Emma was. Damn, she thought. As far as Cam was aware, she hadn't seen her baby niece since yesterday morning. Would he wonder why she hadn't asked after her? She'd had time to ask after Vivien! Would the lapse—as *he'd* no doubt see it—make him wonder if she—Roxy—really cared about her niece? With the great Professor Bergman chasing after her, he must be wondering if she was regretting her decision to marry him and settle down.

With a quiver of her glossy red lips, she handed back the phone. Her spirits had dipped, not only at her lamentable lapse, but at the way Cam... She sighed. What had she been expecting? Some criticism of Vivien? A whispered endearment or two? *Maybe even a tantalising reminder of their coming wedding on Saturday?*

She shrugged off her foolish yearnings. It was hardly a proper wedding. They'd both agreed to a simple ceremony with only Mary and Philomena in attendance—and little Emma, of course. Officially they were both still in mourning, as their friends would understand.

She thanked the receptionist and left the salon, hastening her steps as she headed back to the pharmacy, only to falter as she saw Cam, juggling Emma in one arm and a bulging plastic bag in his other, emerging from the pharmacy where she was supposed to be!

'Ah, there you are!' Cam joined her in a couple of long strides. 'They said they hadn't seen you, and I was beginning to wonder what had happened to you.' He glanced at her empty hands. 'Decided to do some window-shopping first, did you?'

Roxy thought quickly. 'I—um—I discovered that my prescription was out-of-date. But it doesn't matter,' she added hastily. 'It can wait. It's nothing life-threatening.' She gave a quick laugh.

'Well, I'm glad to hear that.' Cam's dark eyes glinted with humour. 'Ready to go? Emma's getting fractious. She's ready for a sleep. Once the car's moving, she'll soon drop off.'

'Like me to take her?' Roxy offered. She was longing to hold Emma again, but didn't want to appear too keen, too anxious.

'If you like.' Cam handed her over with a smile— a faintly surprised, even tenderly approving smile. A smile for Vivien, Roxy thought with a quiver, as she gathered Emma in her arms.

As she looked down at the baby, her niece's small face lit up with a smile.

'Well…you have Roxy's knack for perking up the baby,' Cam murmured as they stepped out into the late-morning sunlight. The clouds had parted earlier, letting the summer sun break through. 'Just look at her…smiling her head off.'

Roxy gave a shrug, as if it was a knack any woman would have. 'Baby's are easily diverted by a new face,' she said lightly, not wanting him to think that Vivien was going mushy over his niece.

As they reached the car the baby began to whimper, wriggling in Roxy's arms. 'Poor little thing, you must be thirsty,' she murmured without thinking.

She was aware of Cam's quick look—the kind of

look he'd often shot at Roxy early on, when she'd done something for the baby that had surprised him. She wondered uneasily if he was beginning to see Vivien as an equally caring mother-figure.

And a more desirable wife?

'There's a small bottle of boiled water and a bottle of milk in the cool box,' Cam told her, opening the car door for her. 'Could you find them while I put Emma in her car seat?'

A few minutes later they were off. It had turned into a glorious day and the rugged coastline, from high above Kiama, looked spectacular...golden cliffs cloaked in rich green, sweeping golden beaches, and deep turquoise water, fringed with a lacy froth of white.

After giving Vivien a glimpse of the Blowhole, which was sending a gushing white spray high into the air from its deep hole in the rocks, Cam turned the car south, heading for the historic village of Berry.

'There are some quaint old buildings here,' he re- marked as they cruised through the village. 'And lots of cafes, craft and antique shops...and a mouth-water- ing bakery. I'll let you nip in and buy something to take back home for our lunch. They have homemade pies and quiches...if your diet allows such things.' He raised a teasing eyebrow at her.

Roxy didn't care what Vivien's diet allowed, or what Cam thought. She was ravenous. 'I'm on va- cation,' she reminded him with a feline arch of her back. 'A quiche, with some salad, sounds just fine.' She glanced over her shoulder, wanting to divert Cam's attention from her to Emma. 'Well, look at that. She's asleep already.'

For some reason, seeing the baby sound asleep in her car seat raised a nervous flutter. It felt, in a jumpy kind of way, as if there were just the two of them in the car now, sitting intimately side by side in the close confines of the car's front seat. Cam must be as aware as she that if either of them moved an inch closer, they would be touching.

Did Cam *want* to touch Vivien?

Much as Roxy was tempted to shift nearer to the passenger door, safely away from him, she made Vivien wriggle just a fraction closer to Cam, until her arm was brushing against his.

Cam didn't show any reaction at all, but he didn't shift away, Roxy noticed. She felt a heady apprehension—an apprehension she'd inflicted on herself!

What was Cam feeling? Thinking? Perhaps secretly *wanting?*

Was tension gripping him? Temptation curling through him? Desire? It was hard to tell.

She lost her nerve and retreated a fraction. Broad daylight, in a moving car, with a baby in the seat behind, asleep or not, wasn't the time to launch into a fullscale seduction scene.

Besides, she wasn't at all sure that she wanted to.

CHAPTER FOURTEEN

IT WAS a relief when Cam drove off to work around 2:00 p.m., leaving her to spend the rest of the afternoon at home alone with Emma. Roxy gave her baby niece an extra big hug and whirled her round in her arms, making her giggle. She kissed Emma on each cheek and told her over and over, in her normal voice, how much she loved her.

With Cam at work, and Philomena having finished her chores for the day and gone home, she could enjoy the baby to the full, without Cam's watchful eye on her, without having to pretend to be Vivien, without having to feel furtive and self-conscious and racked with doubts and misgivings and a quivering nervous tension.

She spent a blissful couple of hours playing with Emma, and when the baby started rubbing her eyes again, she put her niece down for a nap.

With some free time on her hands, Roxy did a re-suscitation job on Vivien, who'd begun to wilt, she realised when she checked in the en suite mirror. Her glossy red lipstick had worn off, her mascara had begun to run, her wig was ruffled, and she had food spots on her tiger-print sweater. It would never do for Cam to see cousin Vivien in this undesirable state!

She examined the few clothes she'd brought with her from town the day before. Since this would be Vivien's last evening with Cam she might as well pull out all stops. She selected a slinky black satin cat suit, which an ex-boyfriend had once given her as a saucy birthday gift—shortly before disappearing interstate with another girl. She hadn't worn it since. She hadn't felt like wearing it—not even to lounge around in at home on her own. But it would be perfect evening leisure wear, she decided, for the flamboyant Vivien.

Once dressed, she went into the dining room and set the table for dinner, using the best silver and the finest glassware, with candles as a romantic touch, ready to light. Dinner was already prepared. It only needed heating. Kindly Philomena had made a pot of potato and leek soup and one of her delicious pasta dishes for dinner. All Roxy—or rather Vivien— needed to do was to throw together a salad and slice some bread. And open a bottle of wine.

Roxy was sorely tempted to make Cam a creamy rice pudding for dessert, but if Vivien presented him with his favourite treat he'd be instantly suspicious. Besides, Vivien wouldn't know how to cook a rice pudding—let alone approve of such calorie-laden food.

Tomorrow night, perhaps, Roxy thought with a sigh of deep yearning. If she survived tonight.

She heard a cry. Emma was awake. As she was about to rush to the baby, she hesitated. What would Vivien do? *She'd protect her slinky cat suit, that's what she'd do.*

She darted along the passage to Roxy's room and grabbed an oversize shirt from a drawer. She was pulling it on as she bounded across the passage to the nursery.

For once Emma didn't stop crying when she saw her. She didn't even sit up. She just held up her hands for Roxy to pick her up. Her cheeks, Roxy noticed in concern, were stained a bright red.

'Teething again?' she murmured as she gathered the baby in her arms and rocked her gently. 'Poor baby. How about a crust to chew on? And a drink of water?'

But soon Emma was grizzling again. Roxy tried everything including a warm bath, but nothing brightened the baby for long. She didn't want to play with her toys. She didn't want to crawl. She just wanted Roxy to hold her.

'Maybe some teething solution on your gums might help,' Roxy said, and carried the baby to the bathroom. Cam needn't know that Vivien had used the solution, or even thought of it. And the baby could hardly talk!

It did seem to help, but Emma still wanted Roxy to hold her. Roxy sank into an armchair in the family room with the baby cradled in her arms, and began to sing all the lullabies she knew...especially Emma's favourite, which had animal sounds—cats, dogs, ducks, cows. It never failed to make the baby smile.

She was so engrossed in her array of animal sounds and so relieved and delighted at Emma's gurgles of laughter, that she was unaware that Cam had arrived home until he strode into the family room midsong.

'Well! You two sound as if you're having fun.' He peeled off his jacket and tossed it into a chair.

'Cam!' She nearly dropped the baby. Had he recognised the song as one that Roxy often sang to Emma? Or didn't men notice such things? Hopefully, if he had recognised it, he'd assume that Roxy and

Vivien, being first cousins and around the same age, must have learned similar songs as children.

She shrugged off her qualms, pulled herself together and switched to Vivien mode.

'Thank heaven you're back, Cam. Emma's been grizzly ever since she woke up. I don't know what's wrong with the poor kid. Missing Roxy, I guess. I've sung every song my mother ever taught me to keep her amused. I even gave her a bath,' she admitted, certain that Cam would see evidence of it. 'And—' she pulled a face '—I was forced to change a dirty nappy. Ugh! Never again! Here...she's yours.'

She handed Emma to him—in a rush, as if glad the baby was off her hands at last—then rose languidly to her feet. Realising she was still wearing Roxy's oversize shirt—hardly Vivien's sexy image—she said in disgust, 'Just look at me! When the baby woke up I ducked into Roxy's room and grabbed an old shirt to cover myself. I'd already changed for dinner, you see, thinking you might be home early.' She sniffed. 'I don't have any big shirts myself—they're so ugly and shapeless.'

Her heart missed a beat. Cam was looking a bit bemused, she thought. Because she was gabbling? Or was he just surprised to see the alluring Vivien in a figure-concealing, oversize shirt?

'It sounds as if you need a break,' he sympathised. 'I'll give Emma her dinner while you take a breather, then I'll take her out to the cliffs to watch the waves—she loves that. After that she can have her bottle and go down for the night...giving us the evening in peace, hopefully.'

He winked at Roxy. No, Roxy thought with a jolt

of unease, he's winking at *Vivien,* not you. 'I noticed
the dining-room table…' His mouth curved in an appreciative smile. 'We're to eat formally tonight, I take
it? By candlelight.'

Roxy gave a saucy toss of her head—then remembered her black wig. She hoped she hadn't dislodged
it. 'Well, I thought, as it's my last night here, we
might as well make it a special occasion.'

'Sure, why not?'

Her heart dipped a little at his ready agreement.
'I'm looking forward to it,' she rallied. She remembered to bat her eyelashes at him. 'It's been such a
domestic day.' She heaved a sigh. 'Domesticity's just
not me. It's so damn boring.' She dropped her voice
a notch lower. 'I feel like letting my hair down a bit.'

She turned away, almost choking on a bubble of
mirth at the idea of letting her hair down. Seeing her
wig flying across the room was the last thing she
wanted!

She swept from the room without daring to glance
back.

The scene was set for seduction. Fine wine, fine food
and flickering candlelight. Romantic violins swirling
from the stereo. A red-blooded man and a sultry brunette, alone together…alone for an entire evening.

Roxy let her eyes smoulder as she gazed across the
table at Cam. If he had any thought of seduction, any
desire to play around with a sexy brunette while his
bride-to-be was away, he would never have a more
perfect opportunity than this. Vivien was openly giving him the green light.

Inside she felt sick. If Cam did succumb to

Vivien's wiles, what on earth would she do? She'd have to take flight before anything too risqué happened. She couldn't risk being unmasked! It would be too humiliating!

She would only wait around long enough for Cam to show his hand, she decided nervously...until he tried to kiss her, perhaps. Just long enough for her to know that her future husband wasn't to be trusted out of her sight.

And what would she—Roxy—do if he did make a pass at Vivien and show that he was incapable of being faithful to the woman he intended to marry? Cancel her plans to marry him on Saturday? Slink back to her flat in Sydney and fight for her niece in the courts? A fight she'd have little hope of winning? Give up her baby niece without a struggle and go back to a career that she'd lost all interest in?

Her heart plummeted at the thought of losing Emma. No! Never! She gazed bleakly into her glass of wine, her mascara-laden lashes hiding the pain in her eyes. She would never give up her niece.

And damn it, she would never give up Cam!

The realisation hit her—painfully. What was an occasional fling on the side, if it didn't mean anything? He'd never promised to love her, but he *had* promised a serious commitment to her. He'd asked her to *marry* him. Even if he didn't love her, he did seem to have a genuine fondness for her, with sexual sparks in abundance when there were no flashy brunettes around.

As long as Cam still wanted her as his wife, as a mother to their baby niece, she would stick to their bargain. She would go ahead and marry him on

Saturday. She would be a loving mother to Emma and a caring, devoted wife to Cam, and hope that in time she might come to mean more to him than—than the dark-eyed, vampish brunettes he found so irresistible!

In the meantime, being forewarned that he was unlikely to be faithful to her would help to fortify her for what lay ahead, giving her a chance to put on a serene front and hide the growing love she felt for him. She wouldn't be so vulnerable then, so easy to hurt.

'Something wrong, Vivien?'

Vivien!

She schooled her features into a dreamy-eyed, heavy-lidded mask before raising her head. 'Just the wine...I'm afraid it's gone to my head. I feel quite tipsy. Quite...' She gave a slow, wicked smile. No matter what the consequences might be, she couldn't let the opportunity slip by! 'Quite wanton.' She ran her tongue over her glossy red lips. 'Let's dance... shall we?'

No man, surely, could fail to read the invitation in her heavily made-up eyes. Eyes as dark and inviting as Mirella's. Eyes as dark and inviting as Belinda's. Eyes as dark and inviting as the stunning brunette at Serena's wedding.

'Certainly...if you wish.' Cam was on his feet before she was.

She felt a tremor as his arm slipped round her waist, sliding over the black satin. His other hand, strong, warm and achingly possessive, swallowed hers. Her nostrils flared as she breathed in the musky maleness of him, her senses spinning as she felt her breasts brushing against his chest. She gulped, unable for a moment to look at him.

The last time—the only time—she'd danced in his arms was the night of her sister's wedding. After tripping over his feet once too often in her impossibly high heels, she'd muttered, 'That's it. I'm taking them off.' And she had, there and then. It had felt deliciously wanton, dancing in her stockinged feet with her sister's sexy best man. He hadn't stepped on her toes once, and amazingly, she hadn't tripped over his.

It was immediately after that highly sensual dance that he'd taken her out into the garden and kissed her—kissed her long and lingeringly, as if it had meant something to him. Only it hadn't. Minutes later, after learning that she spent half her year digging around in the dirt in remote corners of the globe, he'd lost interest and drifted off in search of someone more to his liking.

Her mouth tightened imperceptibly as she swayed in his arms to the slow beat of the music, their bodies close—dangerously close—but their feet barely moving. Which was fortunate, Roxy thought wryly. If she tripped over his feet now, the way she had at her sister's wedding, she could easily give herself away.

Vivien would never trip over a man's feet. She would never be awkward or clumsy. While they kept to this slow shuffle she was safe.

Luckily Vivien was wearing flat-heeled slip-ons tonight.

'Emma likes you,' Cam remarked softly, his lips in her hair. Her synthetic hair, Roxy thought with a quiver of alarm. Would he be able to tell? 'You'd make a good mother, Vivien.'

A good *mother?* Now Roxy really did panic. She
wanted Cam to see Vivien as a steamy seductress, not
as a good mother! What if he saw Vivien as a better
mother than the absent Roxy? A better live-in lover?
A better wife?

'Oh, kids are all right in small doses, I guess,' she
said quickly, assuming a faint shudder. 'But Roxy's
far more caring and patient than I am…she adores
kids. I prefer to have fun…to live…to travel…to be
blissfully free. I'd hate the idea of settling down with
one guy for life. I couldn't stand it. I never intend to
get married…ever. Too stifling. Too boring. I like my
freedom too much.'

She dropped her voice. 'I like excitement…
danger…*fun.*'

Cam shook his head. 'A pity,' he said musingly.
'You've a lot to offer a man, Vivien.' He touched her
cheek with gentle fingertips.

Roxy's heart constricted, a shiver brushing over her
skin at his touch. Was he already succumbing to
Vivien's seductive allure? Already making his first
tentative move? He must know how dangerous it
would be…playing around with Roxy's first cousin.
Did the danger excite him? Did he relish a taste of
forbidden pleasure himself?

Cam was gazing into her face, she realised nervously. 'What's that look for?' she demanded huskily,
hardly caring if it was a question Vivien would ask.
She had to know!

He smiled, tilting his head at her. 'Just thinking
how like Roxy you are, Vivien…apart from those
smouldering brown eyes, of course, and the dark
hair.' He touched the tip of her nose with his finger.

'The same pert nose...' His finger moved down and brushed over her lips. 'The same luscious mouth...' Warm fingers curled round her chin. 'The same small dimpled chin...' He caressed the dimple, ever so gently, with his thumb.

'I'm going to miss you, Vivien,' he murmured, his breath warming her rosehued cheeks. 'Roxy never told me she had such a...bewitching cousin.'

Roxy felt a strangling sensation in her throat, and quickly lowered her eyelashes to hide the flare of alarm in her eyes. *Miss her...bewitching...luscious lips.*

With a superhuman effort she hid the bitter pain that knifed through her.

'She kept very quiet about you, too,' she purred throatily, throwing herself back into her vampish role. 'And I can see why.' She gave a low sexy gurgle, letting her artificially dark gaze sweep over him. 'When Roxy and I were swapping notes yesterday,' she murmured, seeing her chance to find an answer to the question that had been plaguing her the most, 'she gave me a word of warning.'

'Oh?' Cam lifted an eyebrow. 'And what kind of warning was that?'

Roxy gave a throaty chuckle. 'Roxy told me that you were dangerously susceptible to dark-eyed brunettes. You simply can't resist them, she said. Even your brother used to say so, according to Roxy. She warned me to beware of you, Cam.'

'Well...did she indeed?'

He wasn't denying anything, Roxy noted with a deep twinge of disquiet. He was even looking wickedly amused.

'And do you want to…beware of me?' he asked softly, his black eyes challenging her.

Roxy fought down a wave of panic. She'd given him a chance to assure Vivien that Roxy had been mistaken, that his susceptibility to brunettes was a thing of the past, or a figment of Roxy's imagination, but he hadn't. He was actually *flirting* with Roxy's dark-eyed cousin. Actually *encouraging* her advances!

And she had no one to blame but herself! She'd hurtled into this mortifying situation with her eyes wide-open.

Filling her lungs with badly needed air, she gathered her flagging strength. Sorely tempted as she was to reveal herself there and then, to give Cam the fright of his life, she knew that she mustn't. She had to keep up the pretence…the pretence that Roxy was in Sydney selling her flat and that Vivien was Roxy's cousin.

Being exposed as a philanderer—before his wedding day—might incense Cam so much that he might decide to call off the wedding altogether, not wanting a wife who was aware that he played around. He might prefer a more amenable wife. Like Mirella, perhaps.

She couldn't lose Emma now! And damn it, she couldn't lose Cam, either! How could she bear it?

'Poor little Roxy doesn't know me very well,' she breathed huskily—the huskiness from pure nerves this time. 'I took her warning as a challenge. I can't resist a challenge.' She pressed a little closer to Cam, wanting—and yet not wanting—to find out how far he would go, stubbornly ignoring the urge to flee and remain forever unsure of him. She *would* flee…she would have to very soon anyway…but not just yet.

Instead of pushing her away, as she still half-hoped he would, Cam curved his arm more tightly round her waist.

'A challenge?' His lips brushed her hair. Roxy wondered faintly if he preferred Vivien's teased wig to Roxy's soft, natural hair. Her heart was growing blacker by the second. Deep down, she'd hoped… she'd never dreamed…that he would actually make a real pass at Roxy's cousin. Would he have the nerve to go any further?

Yet she couldn't draw back. An irresistible force compelled her to go on.

'What my cousin doesn't know won't hurt her… don't you agree?' she coaxed in a sultry purr, letting her fingers slide up the back of his neck to tangle in the thick dark waves.

'Mmm,' Cam murmured, and her spirits plunged further. But still she couldn't pull away…

'Roxy and I have never been close.' She let her eyelashes flutter seductively. 'We're too different. Poles apart. For all her travels, she's such a prude. So quaint and old-fashioned. She doesn't realise we're swinging into an exciting new millenium, where just about anything goes. She's had her head buried in musty textbooks and dusty digs for far too long.'

She gave a derisive chuckle and trailed her hand down Cam's neck into the hollow of his throat…then let it continue on down, her fingers splaying over the hard muscles of his chest.

'My cousin Roxy believes in marriage and one partner for life.' She injected mild scorn into her voice. 'It's so unrealistic…if you're a red-blooded fe-

male like I am…or a red-blooded male…as I'm sure
you are, Cam.'

She moved her hand downward, across his taut
stomach. If he cared for her at all—for Roxy, not
Vivien—he should be stopping her now.

He didn't.

CHAPTER FIFTEEN

INSTEAD, he swept her into his arms and kissed her—kissed her in a way he'd never kissed Roxy, with a hungry, flaming passion that stopped the breath in her lungs and liquified every bone in her body.

She felt a wave of dismay, devastation, and bitter hurt…even as her body arched against him…even as her breath gasped out, mingling with the heat of his own gulping breaths…even as the scorching fire of his kisses sent explosive currents shaking through her. Her senses felt exquisitely alive, her body was ready to ignite, yet deep down inside her a bitter anger was simmering, a searing hurt, her heart shattering into dozens of jagged pieces.

He wasn't kissing *her*. He was kissing her sexy, dark-eyed cousin. Kissing the vampish Vivien with a savage intensity he'd never shown with Roxy.

She wrenched her mouth away. 'This isn't right!' she gasped, and pushed at his chest until he drew back his head and let his hands slide away.

They faced each other, both breathing heavily, their chests heaving.

'So…' Cam arched a mocking eyebrow. 'You've suddenly developed a conscience.'

A biting pain pierced her. Pity he hadn't developed one first! She bit back the words she longed to fling at him. Vivien wouldn't show that she cared.

She tilted her chin, hoping her red lipstick wasn't

smeared all over her face. In a languorous motion that was classic Vivien, she touched her hair, hoping the black wig hadn't shifted. Her bravado—Vivien's cool bravado—was crumbling fast.

'I must look a mess,' she muttered. Vivien would worry about *that*. The ravishing photographic model, looking less than immaculate, less than desirable. It was a real worry for Roxy, too. It was vital that Vivien's image stay intact.

It was time she made an exit…and fast. It wouldn't look at all out of character for Vivien to scurry off for repairs. Better still, to retire for the night—in smug triumph. She'd tempted Roxy's husband-to-be into surrendering to her sultry charms…and then, just as he was losing control, *she'd* been the one to back off. She could hold her head high.

Unlike Cam.

Did he feel guilty? Humiliated? Remorseful? Roxy hoped he felt all three. Let him wrestle with his own conscience…if he had one!

'See you in the morning, Cam.' She couldn't look at him. The place where her heart had been was a huge black hole. If only she'd never started this pathetic charade!

As she tried to swing away, Cam caught her arm.

'What's the rush, Vivien? Afraid that if I run my fingers through your hair you might lose your wig?'

Roxy's jaw dropped. Don't panic, she thought wildly. It doesn't mean he's recognised you. Lots of women wear wigs. Especially models like Vivien.

She drew on all her reserves of strength to inquire languidly, in Vivien's throaty drawl, 'You can tell that I'm wearing a wig?'

Cam's mouth twisted in the travesty of a smile. 'I'm an expert on brunettes, remember?' His tone was cool, cynical, heavy with irony. But no guilt. No shame. No sign of remorse. His eyes were narrowed and steady, with a coldness in the black depths that chilled her to the bone.

She faced him uneasily. 'I'm a model. All models wear wigs.'

He pulled her closer, grasping both of her arms now, his fingers vise-hard on her soft flesh, lacking any tenderness. 'Why don't you get rid of it…and we can continue from where we left off…mmm?'

He *still* wanted…?

'Cam, I—' She gulped. He was beginning to frighten her. For the first time in Cam's presence she felt threatened…vulnerable…defenseless. She'd allowed Vivien to go too far!

'What's wrong?' His voice was harsh with scorn. 'Afraid to follow through, Roxy?'

She froze. *Roxy?*

Her mouth went dry. He *knew*. He'd recognised her! She sagged in his arms, bitter dismay sweeping through her. She'd failed! Her reckless masquerade had gone up in smoke. Vivien had gone up in smoke. This whole crazy charade had been in vain…a waste of time and effort and nervous energy. Worse, it was so humiliating!

But her hurt went even deeper. 'How—how long have you known?' she whispered. If he'd known who she was *before* Vivien had made her advances… *before* he'd responded to them… A dim hope flickered.

'I think I'm the one who ought to be asking the questions.' Cam's eyes were unreadable, his tone ice-cold. He let his hands drop from her arms as if he could no longer bear to touch her. 'But how about getting rid of Vivien first?' The lips that a moment ago had kissed hers with such blinding passion now held a bitter, coldly contemptuous twist.

'You have five minutes to get rid of that wig and those contact lenses. They were a masterstroke, by the way...they fooled me for quite a while. Your whole clever little act fooled me...but you slipped up, Roxy. You should never have sung that song to Emma...that particular song.'

'It was that? That's *all?*' Just a song...a simple thing like a song! A nursery song that any woman might sing to her child.

But not a woman like Vivien.

'It was enough to start me wondering...looking below the painted surface...thinking back over the past twenty-four hours. And once I had you in my arms...once I felt you, touched you, *kissed* you...I knew.' There was no softening in his tone—none. 'I knew it had to be you, Roxy...and that meant you had to be wearing coloured contact lenses and a wig. Very clever, my dear. Brilliant. Zany, but brilliant. You're quite an actress.' His tone was more cynical than admiring. 'You had me well and truly fooled, didn't you?'

'Cam, if you'd only—'

'Do you want me to pull that wig off you myself?'

She whirled and ran.

When she came back ten minutes later—not at a run this time, in less of a hurry to come back—her face was scrubbed clean of make-up, her hair was her own tousled, sun-bleached mop, badly in need of an expert cut, her blue eyes were visible again and she'd replaced the slinky black satin cat suit with a loose shirt and jeans.

'Well, Roxy...' Cam was still standing where she'd left him—unnerving her anew. 'Now, perhaps, you'll give me an explanation.' He waved her to the sofa and only when she'd sat down did he lower himself beside her—not touching her. His eyes hadn't even wavered as she'd walked in, Roxy had noted painfully. Had she killed any feeling he'd ever had for her?

'So, my dear...what's this devious little game you've been playing? As if I can't guess.' His lip curled, his face granite-hard, with no trace of emotion, not even anger. 'You still can't trust me, can you? You had to find a way to test me...right? A pretty elaborate method,' he taunted coldly. 'Turning yourself into a painted Jezebel...making out you were busy in Sydney...pretending to sell your flat. But still...full marks for ingenuity.'

'But I *am* selling my flat, Cam! That's why I went to Sydney in the first place! And I—I wanted to buy something...something that would *prove* to you that I'm serious about settling down.'

She raised hurt eyes to his. 'I thought you didn't trust *me*...that no matter how often I told you I was home for good, you'd never believe me. I thought you'd always be expecting me to want to go off on more field trips, unless I did something that would *convince* you, once and for all, that I'm back home to stay. That I want to stay *here*...at Raeburns' Nest. V-Vivien was just a—a madcap afterthought.'

She saw a muscle flick at his temple, saw something stir, deep in his dark eyes, saw the cold lips move.

'But you're not up in Sydney selling your flat, Roxy. You're not seeing agents or preparing for prospective buyers. You're *here*. You've been here for two days—dolled up as your imaginary cousin!'

She swallowed. 'Cam, I did hire an agent—the agent who sold us the flat a few years ago—but I left him with a key so that I—I wouldn't have to be there.' She bowed her head. 'I made up the prospective buyers,' she admitted heavily, 'but I'm sure it won't be long...' she trailed off, wishing she'd never thought of masquerading as her cousin Vivien...wishing she'd never thought of putting Cam to the test. It had ruined everything!

Her head jerked up again, her eyes—huge in her freshly scrubbed face—pleading with him. 'Cam, you must believe me! I'll never leave Emma. I'll never leave *you*. I'll never *want* to leave you. No matter how many b-brunettes you have on the side!'

Cam raised a dark eyebrow. 'Brunettes on the side?' He shifted closer, his heavy bulk making a sizable dip in the cushioned seat, almost causing her to topple onto him.

'Roxy, I knew it was you tonight...*before* I made any move on you,' he reminded her. 'I knew before we had dinner. I just wanted to see how far you'd be prepared to go. As Vivien. And perhaps teach you a lesson for fooling me so convincingly. For feeling it *necessary* to fool me.' For the first time the faintest spark of humour lit his eyes.

Roxy bit her lip. 'But—but you are susceptible to brunettes,' she gently accused him. 'I—I've seen you in action, Cam. On—on other occasions.' If she was reasonable about it, maybe he'd be reasonable, too...and assure her that his penchant for brunettes was finally behind him.

Cam sighed. 'If anyone needs to learn about trust, Roxy, it's you...though I'll concede that I might have given you some reason for doubt in the *past*.' He stressed the word 'past'. 'On the two occasions you and I met—at your sister's wedding and at Emma's christening—I attached myself to other women for purely diversionary reasons...for my own self-preservation.'

Roxy's brow wrinkled. 'W-what do you mean?' she breathed.

His chest heaved and fell. 'When I found out at Serena's wedding that you were an archeologist and that you spent most of the year overseas at remote digs, I backed off...deliberately. I knew that if I saw any more of you, got any more involved with you, I'd want to keep you in my life for good. I'd want to marry you...have children with you...keep you here at home with us...and it was clear that you weren't the home-making, settling-down type.'

As Roxy's lips parted, he put a finger to her lips. 'It seemed to me, back then, that you were the last woman in the world I ought to be getting involved with—a footloose, career-mad professional like my wife—like my mother—who'd seldom be there for our children...or for me.'

Roxy's eyes flickered. She caught hold of his finger and gently lowered it from her lips. 'That's why you dumped me for that brunette at Serena's wedding? Not because you were bored with me...or wanted a more glamorous woman in your life…or a girlfriend who'd always be around for you when you felt like a—a bit of fun?'

'No! Roxy, I'm sorry if I hurt you, but it seemed best to end it before it began.' Regret burned in his eyes. 'You and I had been getting on so well at the wedding—things were happening so quickly—that I knew I had to do something about it, and fast. I was afraid I'd already shown my feelings too plainly… maybe even given you…expectations.' His mouth twisted. 'So I backed off deliberately and latched onto someone else…to finish it once and for all.'

He curled his fingers round hers and gripped them tightly. 'I didn't want you waiting around, hoping I'd call, expecting something to happen, getting ideas about us teaming up…if only for short periods at a time, between field trips. I wanted to kill any growing spark between us while I still could. The fact that I couldn't get you out of my mind…well, that was the rod I had to bear.'

Roxy's hand trembled in his, a heady relief washing over her. He hadn't turned to another woman that night because he was fickle…or untrustworthy…or bored with her. He'd wanted to protect himself—emotionally—because he cared *too much,* and because he felt she'd be the wrong woman for him—the wrong *wife.* She swallowed hard. He'd been protecting her, too…not wanting her to wait around for him…not wanting her to expect anything of him.

Cam gave her hand a squeeze. 'The brunette at your sister's wedding, Roxy, was Hamish's tax accountant, Carol.' He smiled gently. 'All I did was drive her home. I wasn't interested in her in any romantic sense. I've never had an affair with her…or wanted one. She was a business acquaintance, simply that.'

'Oh.' Roxy heaved a tremulous breath. There was no need to ask about Belinda, the leggy brunette at Emma's christening. Cam had already told her that Belinda had gone back to her husband. It no longer mattered if she'd been more than a tennis partner to him.

That only left… 'And Mirella? Your secretary?'

'Mirella?' Cam stared at her. 'You never thought—' He gave an amused snort. 'Mirella is definitely not my type.' He raised her hand to his lips and tenderly kissed the tips of each finger. 'In fact, she no longer works for me. I fired her earlier this week. She was drinking too much and her work was suffering…. I've been watching her for some time. I'd already warned her more than once. I've a new secretary now. A…'

Roxy held her breath.

'A sprightly grey-haired widow.' He grinned at her. 'After my experience with Mirella and the man-eating Vivien I'm steering clear of dark-eyed brunettes from now on. Though I must say—' he paused, pursing his lips '—masquerading as a raunchy brunette did bring out a side of you I'd never seen, Roxy. That slinky little black number you were wearing tonight… Wow! I was very tempted to pull down that zipper at the neckline…to pull it all the way down…'

She sat up. 'You *liked* it?'

'Roxy, my sweet, I'd like you in a sack. You even look sexy in that baggy shirt you're wearing. But why hide that gorgeous figure of yours? You should show it off more often.' His dark eyes scorched over her.

'Wear that tarty little cat suit any time you like…as long as you only wear it for me!'

Only for me…

A rosy warmth flashed along her cheekbones. Smiling up at him she asked curiously, 'Were you attracted to Vivien at all…before you knew she was me?'

Cam pursed his lips, and with a roguish grin admitted, 'In hindsight, I'd say there was enough of Roxy in Vivien to stir my body and senses at some subconscious level…but my conscious mind absolutely rejected her…her artificiality…her life-style… her frivolous values. And that over-the-top make-up! Like Mirella, definitely not my type,' he said emphatically.

He pulled her into his arms, settling her in the curve of his shoulder. 'You're my type, Roxy…now and forever.'

Now and forever…it sounded wonderful. She let her eyes glow softly under his gaze, aware that all her tension, all her foolish, unfounded fears, had slipped away. She could look forward to their marriage now…without a qualm. She no longer had any reason to mistrust him…to have doubts about him…to dread the sight of another brunette popping into his line of sight.

Suddenly it no longer mattered that he didn't love her the way she loved him…the way he must have loved his first wife, Kimberley. He'd shown that he felt deeply enough about her to make their marriage work…and to make their life together a happy, warmly fulfilled life. Maybe what he felt for her now would grow in the months and years ahead…maybe even grow into the same deep love she had for him.

Sharing Emma—and perhaps, if they were lucky, sharing children of their own—would surely help.

'I love you, Cam,' she whispered, wanting him to know it. Wanting him to go into their marriage knowing it. 'And I'll always here be with you…for you…as long as you and Emma want me.'

She felt his muscled chest shudder against her. 'We'll want you until the earth freezes over.' He buried his lips in the natural softness of her hair—so different from Vivien's teased wig.

'I still find it hard to believe that my sensible, levelheaded Roxy would go to such bizarre lengths to find out if she's marrying a brunette-obsessed philanderer…' He gave a soft chuckle. 'I can see I'm going to have to be on my toes for the rest of my life.'

She stirred in his arms. 'Cam, I'm sorry I—'

'Hush. *I'm* sorry I didn't trust *you,* my darling.' He looked down at her with tender eyes. 'I have a message for you, by the way,' he added gently. 'Professor Bergman called yesterday to say he'd received your letter…the letter you declined to mention to me.'

She bit her lip.

'I—I was afraid you might think I was putting a gun at your head, Cam, if I told you I'd been invited to a special dig.'

Cam nodded. 'I gathered as much. I take it you refused the dig of a lifetime?' His eyes caught hers. 'The professor asked me to tell you he was really sorry you wouldn't be coming on any more digs in the future.' Emotion glowed in the dark depths. 'But he'd enjoyed working with you, he said, and he understands your decision, "now that you have a family to think about," to quote your own words to *him*.

'You kept this to yourself,' he accused gently. 'To spare *me*. Not wanting me to think that you might secretly *want* to go...'

Roxy shrugged. 'I wasn't tempted for a second. I wrote back immediately, refusing his invitation.'

Cam's jaw clenched. 'I appreciate your sacrifice, Roxy...don't think I don't.'

'Cam, it's no sacrifice—'

'You might not think so now. But I don't want you having any regrets later, Roxy.'

'I won't! I always intended to give up archeology when I married and settled down.'

'Still...you're a bright, intelligent woman with a lot to offer, Roxy. I'm not going to chain you to the house, my love. Here...I've something to show you.'

She glanced up at him, mystified, as he drew back to delve into his pocket.

'I was going to surprise you with it when you came home from Sydney, but since Vivien has departed the scene early...' His smile was wry as he pulled out a newspaper cutting. 'Here...read it,' he said. 'You might be interested.'

She took the cutting and ran her eyes over a heading that made her eyes widen. A *job* application?

She read on. It was an ad for a part-time position as a history lecturer at a nearby college. A knowledge of ancient Mexican and South American history would be an advantage.

Her head snapped up. 'You intended this for *me?*' Cam was urging her to apply for a job outside the home?

'That's right.' Cam bent his head and kissed her on the mouth, his lips tenderly pressing into the softness of hers. 'When you told me you were selling your flat, Roxy, and burning your boats, as it were—closing the door on your old life—I was *concerned* about you, rather than relieved. I was afraid you'd become frustrated in the years to come...and start feeling bitter and resentful that I'd made you give up your career. Not only your field work but your lecturing as well.'

She gazed up at him wonderingly. 'So you looked for a job for me?' she whispered. 'Knowing it would mean that I'd be away from you and Emma for part of the week?'

Cam shrugged. 'When a man loves a woman—deeply loves a woman—he wants her be happy. I've discovered that,' he admitted softly, 'since you've been with me, Roxy.' His lips brushed her earlobe, sending tiny flames flickering through her. *Loves... deeply loves...* 'A man will do anything to avoid losing the woman who means the world to him. He'll do anything to avoid causing her more pain.'

Means the world to him...do anything... Roxy's throat choked up. Cam was finally opening up his heart to her, finally laying his emotions bare, admitting to feelings she'd never known he had...never dreamed he had.

'I want you to be happy, Roxy,' he murmured, 'so I've been looking out for a job that might interest you...and yet not be too far from home. This would be ideal for you...and it's only two mornings a week. Mary or I could look after Emma while you're there. Perhaps you should apply for it, darling. The job doesn't start until college goes back next year.'

He kissed the tip of her nose, then her eyes, ever so gently, first one then the other. 'As for this charade of yours that *I* forced on you, Roxy…dressing up as a vamp to tempt me…it's all my fault, for not telling you how I felt about you…for not telling you I loved you. I was—' He stopped.

'Afraid?' she breathed, reaching up to stroke his rough cheek. 'Why, Cam? Tell me,' she begged.

Cam shrugged, his mouth dipping in a grimace. 'I revealed my feelings too soon to my wife—and she used it against me. She thought that if I loved her enough I'd do anything she wanted—that I'd let *her* do anything her selfish heart desired. But I couldn't agree to live the kind of life she wanted. I didn't love her enough, obviously, or I'd have come to a compromise. But with you, Roxy…'

He paused, trailing his lips down her cheek, burying them in the warmth of her throat. 'I love you enough, trust you enough, to give you the freedom to do your own thing…even to go on a field trip now and then, if you decide you want to. I'd even follow you—with Emma—if you'd let us. When she's a bit older.'

A deep tremor shook through her. Knowing how Cam felt about his mother's abandonment of him as a child, and his ex-wife's callous dismissal of children, she realised what a sacrifice he was making, and how deeply he must love her.

'I don't want to leave you, Cam…ever,' she whispered. 'And I certainly wouldn't want to drag Emma around hot, dusty digs, not even here in Australia. I want to stay here at home with you both…I couldn't wish for anything more. A part-time lecturing job in the vicinity may be a possibility...as long as Emma doesn't suffer. I'll think about it,' she promised, not wanting to throw his loving offer back in his face.

She drew back, a secret smile on her lips. 'But in the meantime I have something else in mind to do in my spare time. I was going to surprise you on our wedding day, Cam...but I don't want any more secrets between us.'

As Cam turned mystified eyes to hers, she said, 'I'll show you now. Wait here.' She flitted off to the guest wing to fetch the books she'd bought in Sydney...the books that had made Vivien's weekend bag so heavy. She staggered back with them.

'There!' She plonked them down on the coffee table and spread them out.

'Gardening books?' Cam stared. One book was on rose gardens, the second on cottage gardens and the third on general gardening.

Roxy chuckled at the look on his face. 'I've always wanted to take up gardening. I've never had a garden—or the time for one. I want to put in a rose garden, Cam—there's not one rosebush at Raeburns' Nest and I love roses. And I'd also like to put in an old-fashioned cottage garden—there are no flowers here, either, other than native flowering shrubs.'

She looked up at him with expectant eyes. '*Can* I, Cam? I always wanted to build a beautiful garden when I gave up field work and settled down. I love digging around in the dirt, as you know.'

He gathered her in his arms. 'If that's what you'd like to do, Roxy...of course you can. A rose garden and a cottage garden at Raeburns' Nest would be marvellous. Perhaps Emma could have a small garden, too, when she's older…so that she can work along-side her mother.'

'Oh, Cam, that's a wonderful idea!' She curled her arms round his neck. 'And I want to have more children. *Your* children, Cam. I want to have the kind of life *you've* always wanted. It's what I want, too. All I'll ever want.'

She gazed up at him with shining eyes. 'I'm sure Hamish and Serena would be happy for us, too,' she whispered huskily. 'I think they secretly hoped we'd get together one day…but I never dreamed it would happen.' Her eyes misted, not with sadness any more but with sheer happiness. 'I love you, Ca—'

His mouth was on hers before she could finish, and then she was lost in the heady wonder of his kiss…thoroughly, comprehensively lost. All thought spun away, reality spun away, his passionate kisses spinning her to the stars, spinning her to the universe, spinning her to the only remote place she would ever want to be.

And Cam—lovingly, knowingly—had taken her there.

MILLS & BOON®

Makes any time special

Enjoy a romantic novel from Mills & Boon®

Presents...™ *Enchanted*™ TEMPTATION.

Historical Romance™ ⊬MEDICAL ROMANCE™

COMING NEXT MONTH

MILLS & BOON®

Enchanted™

KIDS IS A 4-LETTER WORD by Stephanie Bond

When Jo Montgomery found herself having to take three kids to the most important meeting in her career, she was frantic. Then she met the children's father, gorgeous widower John Sterling, and she knew her troubles had just begun...

MARRIAGE FOR MAGGIE by Trisha David

When Devlin Macafferty and his small son literally crash-land onto Maggie's private island, they're both in need of refuge. And as Devlin soon comes to realise, desperately in need of a woman like Maggie too...

THE BABY PLAN by Liz Fielding

Amanda's biological clock was ticking away furiously— and when she met gorgeous Daniel Redford, she began to fantasise about him as the father of her baby. Determinedly, she set her plan in motion. But she hadn't counted on falling in love...

THE BRIDAL SWAP by Leigh Michaels

Had Jax Montgomery's fiancée got cold feet—or was Jax having second thoughts? Either way he needed a replacement bride—and was most insistent that, since he'd hired Kara as his wedding organiser, she must be the one to take on the role...

Available from 7th January 2000

COMING NEXT MONTH

MILLS & BOON®

Enchanted™

A GOOD WIFE by Betty Neels

Matilda tries to ignore her attraction to Dr. Henry Lovell. After all, he's her boss and engaged to someone else! But soon Henry starts to find Matilda just as intriguing as she finds him…

THE BRIDESMAID'S BET by Christie Ridgway

Francesca wanted to get married, so she started taking lessons in seduction from brooding bachelor, Brett Swenson, whom she'd always loved from afar. But once this marriage-resistant man claimed her as his own would he ever see her as a potential bride?

VACANCY: WIFE by Shannon Waverly

Meg's boss had a strict policy to keep romance out of the work place. But, when he took her on a family weekend away, he seemed to see her in a new light. But Meg couldn't allow him to get too close, or he'd discover the secret she'd been keeping from him…

THE LATIN AFFAIR by Sophie Weston

Nicky hasn't allowed a man to get close to her since she was fifteen and a passionate kiss with an older man ended disastrously. How then can she explain her attraction to Esteban Tremain? Is it that he somehow reminds her of that previous moonlit encounter…?

Available from 7th January 2000

MILLS & BOON®

MISTLETOE
Magic

Three favourite Enchanted™ authors
bring you romance at Christmas.

Three stories in one volume:

A Christmas Romance
BETTY NEELS

Outback Christmas
MARGARET WAY

Sarah's First Christmas
REBECCA WINTERS

Published 19th November 1999

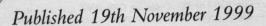

*Available at most branches of WH Smith, Tesco,
Martins, Borders, Easons, Volume One/James Thin
and most good paperback bookshops*

FREE
4 BOOKS
AND A SURPRISE GIFT!

We would like to take this opportunity to thank you for reading this Mills & Boon® book by offering you the chance to take FOUR more specially selected titles from the Enchanted™ series absolutely FREE! We're also making this offer to introduce you to the benefits of the Reader Service™—

★ FREE home delivery
★ FREE monthly Newsletter
★ FREE gifts and competitions
★ Exclusive Reader Service discounts
★ Books available before they're in the shops

Accepting these FREE books and gift places you under no obligation to buy; you may cancel at any time, even after receiving your free shipment. Simply complete your details below and return the entire page to the address below. **You don't even need a stamp!**

YES! Please send me 4 free Enchanted books and a surprise gift. I understand that unless you hear from me, I will receive 6 superb new titles every month for just £2.40 each, postage and packing free. I am under no obligation to purchase any books and may cancel my subscription at any time. The free books and gift will be mine to keep in any case.

N9EC

Ms/Mrs/Miss/Mr ....Initials ....
BLOCK CAPITALS PLEASE

Surname ....

Address ....

....

....Postcode ....

Send this whole page to:
UK: FREEPOST CN81, Croydon, CR9 3WZ
EIRE: PO Box 4546, Kilcock, County Kildare (stamp required)

Offer valid in UK and Eire only and not available to current Reader Service subscribers to this series. We reserve the right to refuse an application and applicants must be aged 18 years or over. Only one application per household. Terms and prices subject to change without notice. Offer expires 30th June 2000. As a result of this application, you may receive further offers from Harlequin Mills & Boon Limited and other carefully selected companies. If you would prefer not to share in this opportunity please write to The Data Manager at the address above.

Mills & Boon is a registered trademark owned by Harlequin Mills & Boon Limited.
Enchanted is being used as a trademark.